An Accidental Legacy

An Accidental Legacy

A NOVEL

Tish Mosley

DILYBU Press Nashville, TN

Published by DILYBU Press
P.O. Box 218441
Nashville, TN 37221
www.dilybupress.com

Publisher's Note: This is a work of fiction. Names, characters, places, and incidents are a product of the author's imagination. Locales and public names are sometimes used for atmospheric purposes. Any resemblance to actual people, living or dead, or to businesses, companies, events, institutions, or locales is completely coincidental.

Book Design by Tip Mosley

An Accidental Legacy/ Tish Mosley. -- 1st ed.
ISBN 978-0-692-75753-6

For the believers

Chapter One

Scots Ridge
Tennessee
January 1968

Thin ice cracked under Sonny Price's bare feet. Running half-naked across the tobacco field dodging the frozen jagged stubs, he balanced his newborn daughter across his arms. The midnight sky, a widow's veil of darkness, loomed overhead in silent judgment. With every convulsion, Melody's tongue clicked in her throat.

Ellis Hatch was changing the 45s on the record player when he saw Sonny coming across the field. He threw open the front door just as Sonny cleared the small porch in two strides. Crossing the threshold, Sonny fell against Ellis sandwiching Melody between them. Ellis felt the heat rising off the baby and smelled the sweat pouring off his friend's bare skin.

Virginia Hatch sat stunned on the couch. Her mouth gaping like a largemouth bass dropped the bobby pins that had been hanging between her lips. The pin curl she was fastening fell like a tangled string in front of her ear.

Ellis placed the baby on a nest of bobby pins in Virginia's lap. She took the baby into her arms and peeled back the pink blanket. Its satin trim smeared with the mud. Melody's eyes rolled back in her head as another convulsion gripped her tiny round body.

"Fever. It won't. Go down." Sonny said panting.

"We've got to get her to the hospital! Ellis get the car!" Virginia ordered and without question Ellis complied.

"What about Kathleen?" Virginia asked looking past Sonny and watching as her husband wearing nothing but the pajamas she gave him for Christmas ran out into the night air to pull the car up to the house. A hot mix of pride and shame flushed her skin. Expecting to see the baby's mother rushing through the opened door, she cut her eyes back to Sonny as if to ask the obvious.

"She's the same. No change. I just..."

Shaking her head to stop him from saying another word. "It's going to be alright Sonny. Some women go through this. She'll pull out. Give her time. Right now, we need to get Melody to the hospital and get this fever down." Virginia said too sweetly for sincerity.

Ellis pulled the car up to the front porch. Sonny jumped in the front seat with Ellis like he had done so many times before even after the two couples had gotten married and Virginia crawled in back with Melody wrapped in her pink blanket and the front of Virginia's housecoat.

Ellis stared at the narrow icy snow packed road across his white knuckles gripping the steering wheel. He swallowed hard trying to dislodge his confidence stuck in his throat like a walnut. It was up to him to get them down the ridge to the hospital. He followed the Impala's headlights like two yellow arms grabbing at the shiny white ribbon of road. A wall of darkness pressed in on every side. Ellis felt guilty for wanting to be in his bed like everyone else on top of the ridge tucked in warm for the night, their bellies full of leftover Christmas ham and Red Velvet cake. It would suit him just fine if he never had to leave Fulton. It had been his home for the past twenty-one years and had everything and everyone he needed.

The car fishtailed twice as Ellis eased it around tight curves that snaked through Shepard's Gap and over the steep drop into Pig's Eye Hollow. As the road flattened out, they each exhaled and began panning up ahead in hope that the ice wasn't as bad at the bottom of the ridge in Tillman. Familiar houses like living mile markers between the life they lived on top of the ridge in Fulton and that of Tillman at the bottom of the ridge, looked like dark brooding monsters. Some houses still had their Christmas trees in the front windows. Some were lit looking like cheap imitations of happiness. Others leaned against the glass as cold and dark as the night.

The neon beer signs at the Red Stagg Tavern glowed from their black cords filling Ellis and Sonny with sticky contrition. Without its bright lights and swollen parking lot, it was just another rundown cinderblock building in need of paint.

Virginia's gaze fell on the tavern too but her reaction was the same as always. Disgust. She saw the tension swell in her husband's shoulders but forgiveness was never her strong suit. Turning her attention to the baby, Virginia rocked from side to side humming a broken hymn. She was trying to comfort the baby and herself. The slow creep along the icy roads was making them all nervous. Silently they feared they wouldn't make it in time. Especially Sonny. All his life he felt like time was shorter for him. As if God had forgotten him. He watched how easy life was for others. As if they had all the time in the world. But not him.

He remembered waking to the sound of Melody's tongue clicking in the back of her throat as if she was drowning in her bed. Rushing to the bassinette in the corner of his and Kathleen's bedroom, he panicked when he saw her body bowing with each convulsion. Reaching down to take her in his arms and feeling the heat burning her from the inside out making her almost too hot to touch, he did what he always did. He ran.

Looking over his shoulder into the backseat seeing the two of them back there, Sonny felt an old sour sickness in his stomach leach into his bones.

"There Ellis at the next light." Virginia gave direction as if none of them had ever been to town.

"Yes ma'am!" Ellis quipped and then regretted it. "Think there's room beside the ambulance?" Ellis asked but goosed the gas sending the Impala up the small rise from the street to the emergency room door and parked between the door and the ambulance before anyone could answer.

Semple Conners had worked the swing shift since she took up nursing thirty years in July. The gray bags under her eyes matched the color of her hair making her starched uniform appear whiter than it was under the florescent lights. Sipping coffee and reading yesterday's newspaper at the registration desk, she jumped to her feet when she heard the commotion. Her gold nametag had fallen forward and was lying face down on her left breast that rested atop her large belly leaving a pucker where her right breast once was. Looking across her black frame glasses with their gold chain tucked into the rolls and creases of her neck, she didn't give Virginia time to explain. Instead Semple grabbed Virginia by the elbow with a grip like eagle talons and parted the metal double doors that separated the waiting area and the emergency room with her massive body.

Ellis in his candy cane pajamas and Sonny in blue jeans stood barefooted staring at the metal doors expecting them to part delivering someone to tell them what to do next.

"Coffee sounds good. What do you say? It'll warm our bones." Ellis feeling uncomfortable with the silence patted Sonny on the shoulder. It was his nature to keep things light hearted no matter how bad things got. But Sonny was lost in thought and never heard him. After a few minutes of silence and no sign of the nurse, Ellis decided to walk off his pent up energy. He knew Virginia wouldn't appreciate him walking away and would find something to be embarrassed about but Ellis had long since learned to push Virginia's voice to the back of his mind. He wasn't concerned about being in pajamas and didn't think anyone else would give him a second glance considering most of the people in the place were dressed just like him.

Left alone and lost in a world of thought and misery, Sonny was too tired to hide the fear and frustration across his face and down the hard lines of his body. His mind was swimming. Backstroking over the last few weeks and getting lost in the dark murky waters of his past.

It had only been three weeks since Melody was born. She came with the ice storm. They were all stranded at home. When Kathleen's water broke, Ellis and Sonny headed down the ridge in Ellis's old Chevy, the one parked outside the emergency room door, and made it about half way down the first hill when the car left the road getting stuck in a ditch and they had to go on foot the rest of the way. By the time they made it to Dr. Kirby's house on Maddox Chapel, halfway down the ridge, Kathleen was in full blown labor and the baby was coming fast.

Ellis and Sonny helped Doc Kirby hitch his mule to his wagon and back up the ridge they came just minutes before Melody made her entrance into this world.

Sonny and Ellis waited outside on the porch just about freezing to death after their walk and ride in the wagon but there was little room for them and their hooting and hollering, cigar smoking and passing the jar inside the small house. Virginia said when the doctor handed the baby girl to Kathleen that if she lived to be a hundred years old she would never forget the excitement of bringing this little one into the world. Little did she know that only three short weeks later there would be more excitement with Melody as she lay somewhere behind the heavy metal doors of the county hospital emergency room burning with a fever and convulsing.

Sonny played it all back in his mind. Kathleen reeling in pain as the birthing pains came on suddenly. The ice storm that had covered the ridge the night before leaving everything in a solid sheet of ice. The ice pellets that continued to fall throughout the day as the sun hung low in the sky never offering to warm the day above freezing. His old car up on blocks, its radiator busted and battery dead. Desperation surrounded him. His only hope was his childhood friend and neighbor Ellis Hatch. Ellis was there any time Sonny needed him and he didn't disappoint this time as well. As grateful as Sonny was for Ellis's good nature and willingness to lend a hand, he had a family depending on him now and he needed to know he could provide for them no matter what was needed.

Sitting in the sparse emergency room waiting area. The walls closing in on him like a vice. Sonny's desperation got the best of him. He needed to find a way out. He didn't know how to bring Kathleen out of her sadness. He didn't understand it. Was she unhappy with him? Was she unhappy about the baby? Did she want to leave him and live in town? Was it being on the ridge? He had to make her happy. That was the one thing he promised her. Promised her mama and daddy. Promised God. But how was he going to do that. And, then Melody coming along and neither one of them saw her getting sick. She went from cooing one minute to burning with a fever the next. It was too frightening to watch. He didn't know how to care for a baby. He had never been around babies until he had one of his own. Kathleen was no help. Rolled up in the bed covers. Turned to the wall as if life as she once knew it had never existed. What was he to do? Where could he turn? Who had the answers he needed? Sonny wrestled with fear and doubt until his exhausted mind snapped. Without saying a word he got up and walked out. He left the county hospital emergency room waiting area, walked out the door he had just rushed through with his sick baby girl, walked around to the driver's side door of his best friend's car, and got in. He got in, turned the keys left in haste in the ignition, pulled the gearshift on the column into reverse and backed out of the parking lot as if he had been there during regular visiting hours.

Virginia reached the window of the emergency room door just in time to see Sonny pulling out of the parking lot and driving out into the darkness. She had been standing behind him. She knew she had said too much but he acted like he hadn't heard a word. Filled with regret and guilt she hugged the mud stained pink blanket.

Chapter Two

The Impala slid on the ice as Sonny wrestled the steering wheel to keep control. He had lost complete control of his life. He wasn't about to lose control of the car. He needed help. His wife lay in their bed lost in a world of her own making. He couldn't pull her back among the living. She had been going on and on for months about how things would be different when the baby came. He knew she was miserable living in Mud Flats. He was too. The solemn promise he made to himself as a kid, that if he ever made it out of that three mile hollow he would never go back, shamed him. But like a dog going back to its vomit, Sonny's desperation sent him back to the only place he knew.

Rounding hairpin turns on ice as slippery as snot, Sonny didn't see the doe as she leaped over the guardrail. A flash of brown and then a hard pitch from the right was all the car needed to send it across the invisible double yellow line, through the small opening in the guard rail, over the edge and down the ravine. Pines and cedars snapped like toothpicks over the car's front end sending them flying like missiles to land in the deep tire tracks. Sonny did his best to hold on. There was nothing more he could do. The car was moving too fast and with no traction. Deeper and deeper the Impala bounced and skidded in the snow and ice through the thick underbrush, felling trees and scrapping beds of frozen limestone. The last thing he saw was a shadow, as black as coal, drop down the back windshield. The pale gray moonlight lost at the top of the ravine.

Virginia stood at the emergency room door waiting for Sonny to return. At first she thought he had gone out for some air. Never one to sit indoors for long, she knew Sonny was sure to find his way outside before there was news about Melody. Ellis had long since lost his way somewhere in the hospital. She was certain of it. She figured he had ran into someone he knew and was visiting, as was his habit, leaving Virginia alone to wait.

That was married life as she knew it. She had long since come to accept it.

Suddenly, the glass in the door pulsed. Virginia placed her hand on the glass foolishly hoping it would do it again. The glass slightly trembled against her palm. Two men in white raced passed her. They jumped into the parked ambulance. The lights spinning. The siren echoing.

"Virginia! Virginia Jean! Where's Sonny? I need to talk to him about the baby." Semple scolded. She had been calling out to Virginia asking where Sonny was but Virginia was so rattled by the sudden explosion of activity, in the otherwise quiet hospital, she didn't hear Semple calling out her name.

"He's ah...he's ah...I don't know. He was here. And, then he wasn't."

"Virginia this isn't a time for silliness. You've got to tell me where Sonny is."

Virginia bristled at being called silly. She was many things but silly was not one of them. She squared her shoulders, wrapped the loose strand of hair behind her ear and with her most grownup voice she explained that Sonny had left. Without explanation, without a word, he walked out of the hospital, got in her husband's car and drove away.

Semple tucked her chins deep into the folds of her neck and studied the linoleum floor for a second or two collecting her thoughts.

"Well, I need to explain things to someone. You'll have to do."

"Humph."

"This isn't a time for pride Virginia Jean. There's a baby in there that needs tending. With no sign of a mama or a daddy here to tend to her, that leaves you."

Virginia's pride went from bruised to puffed-up. Once again, as she was often heard saying, she was the responsible one. Instead of being pulled by the elbow, she followed the swish-swish of Semple's girdle, back into the emergency room.

Virginia kept her head down as a show of respect but her curious eyes studied the scenes between each curtained space as she passed by. Nurses tending to the sick and injured glanced in her general direction hearing footsteps pass but didn't make eye contact. Their work, more important than a silly suspicious girl, kept them focused and distant.

Semple stopped outside of one of the curtained spaces. Turning to Virginia, she held the curtain in one hand, and with the other she pointed.

"Virginia, this baby is sick. Real sick. If you had waited any longer, we'd be standing at Bishop's Funeral Home right now instead of the county hospital."

Virginia swallowed the hard knot of emotions. She fought back tears. Embarrassed she didn't want to be the one in charge. But she had no choice. Her heart beat hard in her chest. Her knees buckled soft and just before she selfishly gave way to the urge to pass out, Semple snapped her fingers and Virginia's back stiffened. She nodded. Submitting.

* * *

The county fire engine and ambulance blocked the road keeping any passing car or curious neighbor from getting too close to the crash scene. Flames shot up out of the frozen woods like roman candles. Too hot for the three fire fighters to approach, and with the only hydrant another six miles up the ridge, the best they could do was to let it burn itself out and pray for the best. The two ambulance workers readied the stretcher for any casualties and someone radioed the coroner just in case. Ruskin Bright, Jessup County's Sheriff, parked on the opposite side of the road and made his way over to the scene. The ice wet and treacherous made walking next to impossible.

"Boys, what do we got here?" Ruskin asked waiting for anyone within earshot to answer as he looked around surmising the situation. Woke from a dead sleep by dispatch reporting a car left the road on the ridge was not something that would normally send his stomach into summersaults. It wasn't uncommon anytime of the year for someone to lose control over the narrow pass and find themselves a foot or two over the edge. But when he heard the fire engine and ambulance was dispatched, it was more than his nervous stomach could handle. He needed to throw up. Burning bile blistered his throat but he refused to embarrass himself. It was bad enough he got there last but to lose his stomach was a sign of weakness. With all that lay before him, plumes of flames three stories high, the smell of rubber burning, and the sound of glass shattering, Ruskin knew it would be him and not anyone else that would soon be sitting at kitchen table explaining that someone wasn't coming home. Someone was driving that car when it left the road. And, by the looks of things, that someone was gone for good.

"We've got a dead deer about a hundred yards off the side here. Looks like she may have caused the accident. The blood trail follows from there to there." Denny Bishop, Morgan Bishop's oldest boy, explained pointing the barrel of his flashlight from the small red puddle on the side of the road to the red dotted trail over the snow and ice and down the ravine.

"You boys letting her burn out?" Ruskin asked.

"Yeah, too hot to approach. Whoever it was. Well..."

Denny and Ruskin shook their heads in disbelief and in respect. Like Ruskin, Denny had seen his fair share in his time working for the county fire department. Growing up the oldest son of the owner of Tillman's only white funeral home, he knew the inevitability that followed an accident like this.

"Anyone radio dispatch to call the coroner?"

"Yeah, Birdwell's on his way."

"Shame, just a crying shame folks can't stay off the roads when the weather gets like this."

"Guess they had someplace to be? Would have to be an emergency to get me out on a night like tonight."

They each exhaled a nervous laugh in agreement.

"Well, boys we need to get on with it. Let's get down there as soon as we can. We'll need to identify the vehicle and contact next of kin."

Denny nodded knowing it gave Ruskin comfort to say we, knowing all the while, the responsibility fell squarely on Ruskin's shoulders. The others were there to do a job too but Ruskin's wouldn't end when the hoses were back in place and the fire truck was back in the fire hall. Denny had the utmost respect for Ruskin Bright but it was on nights like this that he wouldn't trade places with him for love or money.

Chapter Three

Virginia stared at the little life lying wrapped in a hospital blanket. On the bedside tray, pushed out of the way, was a wash pan of melting ice. Floating under the ice, a white washcloth with the hospital's blue ink stamp. The same blue ink stamp that was the blanket. The same blue ink stamp that reminded Virginia who was in charge.

A young man with flushed cheeks wearing a white doctor's coat stood by the bed. He was reading Melody's chart, making notes, things Virginia wouldn't understand if he explained them a hundred times in words of one syllable. But it didn't take a medical school education to see that Melody was very sick.

"It's an infection. We've caught it but she's not out of the woods. Not by a long shot." He said as he hugged the clipboard with its yellow and green and white pages filled with squiggly handwriting to his chest. "She's going to need attention. Around the clock attention, do you understand?"

"Yes, sir. I understand." Her voice cracked with emotion. She didn't understand. Did this mean she would be taking care of Melody? Nursing her back to health? She had no idea the cause of Melody's illness and she was not a relative. She had no idea if Sonny, wherever he ran off to this time, would want her to interfere with Melody's care. And, there was Kathleen to consider. Who was taking care of Kathleen? Virginia? Was all of this, all of Sonny Price's problems, raining down on her? And, where was Ellis in all of this? Virginia had, a child of sorts, of her own. She knew Ellis would agree on the front end, because that's just what Ellis Hatch does. He is all in with any new scheme or plan and willing to help out, like tonight going the extra mile for Sonny Price, but when it inches in on the time and attention Ellis expects from people. People like her, his wife, then there will be hell to pay and it will be Virginia writing the check.

"Now, we need to get her prescription. I don't expect

you to have to try to fill it tonight. God knows we don't need to wake the whole town. So, I'm giving you what she will need. If she's not showing improvement." He paused to wait for comprehension to spread across Virginia's face. "Bring her in. Don't wait. Do you understand?"

Virginia felt the heat of shame flood her body from head to toe. She knew the doctor was right. His judgment was right about Melody's care. And, his judgment was right about her. There was nothing she could do to change his judgment to mercy. She felt it sink deep. It would ring in her ears that way for the rest of her life. No amount of consolation could erase the humiliation she felt at this very moment.

"I understand." Virginia mumbled under her breath.

"A nurse will be in directly with the discharge papers."

"Her father...he's..."

"Is he not in the hospital?"

"No. He...he left."

The doctor hung his head in frustration. He summed up the course of events that brought the baby to the emergency room. He had no choice but to release his patient to this disheveled and ill-equipped person.

Exhaling to collect his thoughts and guard his words, "You sign for the father. I'll take care of the rest."

"Alright." Virginia said worried about what more had to be done.

Tenderly the doctor brushed the cooled brawl of the baby, patted her tiny tummy and walked out of the curtained room leaving Virginia on her own.

"Okay, Honey, here's your prescription. Take it as it says on the label making sure to take it all even if you get to feeling better." The nurse said as she came through the parted curtains. Her hair the color of a yellow crayon tucked tight under her stiff white hat with its funny points where ears would be if she were a cat. Virginia thought how smart the hat made the nurse look.

"I'm not the patient." Virginia corrected.

The nurse laughed under her breath leaving Virginia to

wonder if she was laughing with her or at her. It was always the same in Tillman. It was common knowledge anyone raised up in Tillman thought they were better than anyone living or dead on top of the ridge. Virginia could count on both hands the number of places she'd live on the ridge before she'd ever think of living in Tillman. She didn't know this nurse. But that didn't matter. They both were standing in Tillman and that made her better.

"The directions are the same, Honey, no matter who the patient is. Just follow the directions and everything will be just fine." The nurse gave one last glance to the baby sleeping on the smooth white sheets, rolled her eyes down Virginia, handed Virginia her pen and pointed where to sign.

Virginia felt small and insignificant. In spite of it being the middle of the night, when most women in town would be in their gown, Virginia felt underdressed and ridiculous. Her scalp tightened from the tension building in her body pulling tight the pin curls covering her head. Like a reflex, she patted her head feeling the bobby pins, remembering the interruption and why she looked the way she did. Hot tears stung her raw eyelids. She couldn't hold them back any longer. The embarrassment was overwhelming. She envied Sonny for running away.

Virginia was determined not to say another word in front of this snooty nurse. She signed Sonny's name and handed the pen back to the nurse who turned and left through the part in the curtains. Her soft soled shoes squeaking against the waxed linoleum floor.

"Come on sister girl, we need to get you back to your mama. Lord only knows where that daddy of yours has ran off to."

Virginia fastened the top button on her housecoat, pushed her feet deeper into her house shoes, and picked up the baby along with a hospital blanket folded at the foot of the bed daring anyone to ask her about it. She reached for the bottle of pink medicine, shoved it into the pocket of her housecoat and walked out of the emergency room like she was walking out of church.

"Excuse me ma'am. Can you tell me if a tall man in pajamas has been through here?" Virginia raised her free hand up in the air showing Ellis's approximate height. The shift change deposited a cheerful nurse at the registration desk, a world of difference from Semple Conners. Eager to please, she stood and pointed down the hall.

"I saw a man come through here just two seconds ago. Look around like he had lost something, and take off back down the hall towards the cafeteria."

Virginia summoned a weak smile of gratitude and turned to find a place to wait.

* * *

Ruskin eased his way down the embankment. The batteries in his flashlight were dying causing the ribbon of light spilling from it to drop from sight just when he needed it the most. Twice he lost his footing and slid down through the underbrush covered in six inches of snow and ice. The snow had been lying for a week and if he believed old wives tales, there would be more.

"Look out!" Jimbo Cunningham came sliding down behind Ruskin. At twenty-two and thin as a rail, little slowed the young deputy when he too lost his footing on the steep hillside. "Mac's on his way down!" Jimbo yelled as he stopped short of plowing into a tree.

"This is not the time to be messing around boys." Ruskin said. Cold and wet and worried about what he would find, Ruskin reeled in his two deputies. His impatience with their youth and inexperience got the best of him. Brushing the snow off the seat of his pants and struggling not to lose his footing again, Ruskin stood on the slope of the ravine forcing his imagination and years of experience to piece together the accident scene through the patchy darkness.

"As best we can tell, looks like a deer cut across the road just as the car was coming over the top and around the bend. The doe is laying about a hundred yards that way." The two young deputies followed the line of Ruskin's arm taking into consideration his every word. "And from the looks of these snapped trees and shallow tire tracks, he must have been traveling at a high rate of speed when he topped the rim." The deputies shown their flashlights this way and that to take in the full picture of everything their boss described. Ruskin's flashlight flickered in his hand casting cryptic messages onto the snow.

"Weather's turning worse. We got any help getting this car out of here?" Jimbo asked.

"Not today, son. We'll have to leave her here for now. Our first job tonight," Ruskin looked in the starless sky and corrected himself, "might as well as say morning. Is to retrieve the bodies and identify them. I'll then have to contact the next of kin."

Both deputies dropped their heads out of respect for the dead and the task that lay before their mentor. Flames from the burning car casting an orange glow on everything and everyone in sight. No one wanted this part of the job, but if anyone could handle it with grace, it would be Ruskin Bright. For Jimbo and Mac, working for Sheriff Ruskin Bright was one of many reasons they decided to join the sheriff's department. But Ruskin, was the only reason they stayed.

Ruskin moved closer to the burning car and approached the driver's side. "Nothing. There's no one here." He shouted back to the others. They each looked at one another as their shoulders fell in relief but disbelief took its place. It was almost too hard to comprehend that someone could have survived. Ruskin walked all the way around the fiery scene careful not to disturb any tracks that may be left by the driver or passengers. He wrote down the license plate number and motioned for the others to join him.

"Boys, we need to look around. Could be they were ejected. As fast as he was coming down this ravine and by the looks of the tree that stopped him, we could have bodies tossed about."

The group fanned out to search for bodies. For survivors. An hour or two passed as each circled back to the site having seen nothing to report. Ready to take another run at it they had to call off their search as a mix of snow and ice began to fall through the leafy canopy filling the holes their feet had made.

Back upon the road, Ruskin thanked everyone for their quick response and dedication to their respective departments and Jessup County. He made arrangements with the two deputies to return to the crash site once the weather cleared. They each went their separate ways. Riding in silence. The wipers brushing falling ice and snow to the side as they pushed aside thoughts of the fire. No one wanted to be the first to say they recognized the car.

Ruskin sat in his driveway listening to the engine idle and the static on the radio. It settled his nerves. Dread wrapped its arms around him. Giving him that familiar squeeze. The one that pushed him. Pushed him to keep going. He watched through the picture window, as his wife, Florence, moved around the kitchen preparing breakfast. Thirty years of marriage and routine recreated the sounds and smells of what he was seeing from the warm car.

The bubbling percolator and the enticing smell of coffee brewing. The clatter of the tin sifter against the lard stand Florence kept the flour in. The soft tap of her wedding band on her floured hand against the side of the sifter as the last bit of flour dusted the white mound on the table. His body relaxed as he watched her slow graceful movements prepare a pan of biscuits from the dough she mixed with her bare hands just like the generations of women before her. The gentle scrape of her fingernails as she slid the biscuits from her palm to the aluminum, baking pan. The wet plopping of the eggs being whisked with a fork as Florence held the bowl like a baby close to her breast. The bowl turned up on its side tempting the swirling yellow mixture to leap over the edge. Ruskin could sit there in his vinyl-lined cocoon all day and watch from a distance as his wife went about her daily chores but his stomach was empty and his day was full.

Breaking the static, he radioed his location, turned the keys in the ignition and went inside.

Chapter Four

Florence stood in the kitchen. Her face flushed from the heat of the oven. "It's dispatch." She said holding the avocado green phone receiver out to Ruskin just as he came through the front door. He sighed and took the phone receiver from her giving her a quick kiss on the cheek.

"Bright here." Ruskin cleared his throat.

"Sheriff, sorry to bother you at home." Ivy Moore, Jessup County dispatcher, apologized.

"No need for that, Ivy. You're just doing your job. What's this about?"

"Ran those plates. The ones from the burned out car."

"Yeah. What'd you get?"

"Sheriff, you're not going to believe this."

"Ivy, at this point I'm not sure I'll believe anything but I can't if you don't spit it out."

"The car is registered to Ellis Hatch. Ephraim and Mildred Hatch's boy."

Ruskin's knees buckled as he repeated, "Ellis Hatch." Florence motioned for him to sit and he complied without hesitation. He had known the Hatch boy since he was born. He had grown up with Ram Hatch. Ran the roads with him. Worked the fields with him. Now, he had to tell him this bad news.

"But Sheriff here's where it gets sort of crazy."

"Crazy? What are you getting at?"

Ruskin's mind had already jumped too many steps ahead. In his mind, he was no longer on the phone with Ivy. Instead, he was in the Hatch living room. Sitting knee to knee with Ram and Milly ready to bow their heads in prayer and ask God's favor on their son.

"Ellis Hatch is at the hospital."

Ruskin's head began to spin with the shift in details. His face had gone pale. He braced himself as Ivy slowly relayed the information to him.

"About the time we got the call back on the registration, a call came in from the hospital from Jules Caster. Said, when he got back to the hospital he noticed the car that had been parked by the ambulance before he got called out to the accident scene was no longer parked at the emergency room door. Said, he had noticed it earlier and said to someone it looked like Ellis Hatch's car. He said he was about to go check to see if something had happened to Virginia was the reason why Ellis had parked right up at the emergency room door, when the call came in about the fire on the ridge. Jules said when he got back there stood Ellis and Virginia Hatch in their bed clothes looking right as rain but the car was nowhere to be found."

"Did Jules say who Ellis thought may have taken his car?"

"Yep, said it was Sonny Price. Said Virginia saw him drive off in it. Said she didn't think too much of it at the time knowing how Sonny can't sit in one spot for long. But, when he didn't come back and then she saw the ambulance tear out not too long after Sonny had left. Well, Sheriff, she sort of put two and two together. I think we all can."

"No need jumping to conclusions just yet Ivy. Do you know if Ellis and Virginia are still at the hospital?

"Yes Sir. At last report, they are still there."

"Alright, I'm heading over there to discuss this with them. If you should hear from Jules or anyone from the hospital, tell them to have Ellis and Virginia stay right there. I'm on my way."

"Yes Sir."

"Oh, and Ivy?"

"Yes Sir?"

"Why were they at the hospital?"

"The baby. Sonny and Kathleen Price's baby. Fever."

Ruskin cleared his throat again and hung up the phone. There was no need explaining anything to Florence. She had heard enough one-sided conversations over the years to know this was not a time for questions.

"I've filled a thermos with coffee." Florence said as she

rolled the top down on a brown paper sack and placed the thermos on the kitchen table in front of Ruskin.

"There's half a dozen ham and biscuits in here. That should hold you until later today but I'll have a plate ready at eleven like always. If you're here, it'll be waiting on you. If not. Well, we'll cross that bridge when we get to it." She said as she took his cap off his head and gave his hair a quick comb through with her fingertips. It was one of her many ways of saying I love you.

Ruskin stood and for the length of several heartbeats, he clung to his wife and tried to memorize the feel of her. The smell of her. The sound of her. Reassuring him.

With the thermos under his arm and the paper sack heavy with warm biscuits, he left their home like he had so many times before with no idea what he was up against and no idea when he would be walking back through the front door.

Florence sat at her kitchen table alone. The pale winter sun was spilling from the window over her kitchen sink filling her cookie cutter kitchen with soft shades of pink and yellow. She didn't want to think about what had pulled her husband away from their warm bed in the middle of the night. She didn't want to think about the other side of the phone conversation and the people involved. Like Ruskin, she had a lifetime of memories built over the years with Ram and Milly Hatch. Her mind swam with all that she could do but knew she couldn't overstep Ruskin's work. It was a tightrope she walked.

Chapter Five

Lost in thought, Florence raked biscuit crumbs around her plate with her fork making sugary trails of peach syrup from the warm peaches that had covered her buttered biscuit. Like the coffee ring on her Formica kitchen table, the one-sided telephone conversation circled in a continuous loop in her mind. She knew it would spin until she was able to fit all the missing pieces together. And, she knew from experience, anything involving Ellis Hatch would without a doubt include Sonny Price.

Florence had lost count the number of times Ruskin had been called out in all hours of the day or night over the years because of some sort of trouble with Sonny Price. Sonny may not have started the trouble but he always was in the middle of it. There were times she wasn't sure if she felt sorry for Ruskin or Sonny. To her it felt like neither had a choice. Ruskin was just doing his job. And Sonny. Sonny was a Price. And, a Price always meant trouble. She remembered her Granny saying most snakes crawl on their bellies unless they are a Price. Florence liked to believe she was fair minded and didn't pass judgment but many times she caught herself too quick to judge when the trouble involved Sonny Price.

"Knock! Knock! Anyone home!" Goldalena Filbry said as she walked in politely pecking on the front door.

"In here Miss Goldie!"

"Coffee smells good."

Florence poured her neighbor a cup of coffee. Added cream the way she liked it without being reminded. And, set out a plate, fork and knife for Goldie to help herself to the biscuits and peaches. Goldie wasted no time complying. Draping her husband's wool coat over the kitchen chair near the stove to dry. She pulled out a handkerchief from the back pants pocket just as Judge Filbry had done for years, tucked it into one of his flannel shirts, worked his belt buckle in place as to not have the pointed corners jab her in the belly like she had seen him do so many times before sitting down to a meal.

Fifteen years ago, Florence would have commented on the fine ensemble in an effort to comfort the grieving widow, but like everyone else in Jessup County, she had become accustom to Goldie Filbry wearing her dead husband's clothes.

"Ruskin not here?" Goldie stated the obvious between bites of biscuit.

"No ma'am. He's had to run up to the hospital."

Goldie Filbry's eyes widened. Her thin lips dropped open spilling biscuit crumbs. And just before she could ask yet another obvious question Florence assured her Ruskin was not injured or sick.

"Well, I figured it couldn't be Ruskin." Goldie said.

Florence smiled. Knowing her neighbor knew more than she let on. She always did. The oldest person in the neighborhood. Goldalena Filbry had lived her sixty-two years earning the reputation of a busy body. She was aware of the rumors and did nothing to dissuade folks to the contrary.

"Hospital you say."

"Yes ma'am"

"Wonder if it had anything to do with that boom I heard just before dawn."

"Boom?"

"Surely you heard it?"

"No ma'am. Must have slept right through it."

"Woke me right up. Can't go back to sleep after something like that. Curious thing is right after I heard the boom. Guess it was, oh I'd say about ten minutes or so, no more than that. I heard my cellar door."

"Your cellar door?"

Florence did her best to keep the conversation from Ruskin's work but her curiosity was piqued. Goldie sensed it as she helped herself to more coffee.

"Could have been the wind. I reckon."

Florence looked out the window over her kitchen sink. The snow had slowed to flurries and a fresh blanket of white lay smooth across her backyard except for where it fell in the dog pen. Ruskin's bird dogs were playing in it like children.

"Doesn't look too windy out there. Are you sure it was the wind?"

"Well, what more could it have been?"

Goldie had her suspicions about her cellar. She had seen the dark figure run from the back of her house away from the cellar door to the tree line on the back side of her property. It was the edge of the woods that ran up the south side of the ridge. She knew the explosion she heard came from on top of the ridge. And, she saw the flames shoot out of the bare treetops just before dawn. She had heard the fire truck's siren and saw the red light strobe the sky. She heard the ambulance too and saw when Ruskin had left driving in the direction of the commotion.

Florence played back the one-sided telephone conversation. She didn't remember Ruskin saying anything about someone being on the run. Mentally she ticked off the details. Ellis Hatch. Missing car. Virginia. Hospital. If Ruskin was concerned that Ellis and Virginia might leave the hospital before he got there, what was all that about a car missing? Did he say it was Ellis's car? Did he say why they were at the hospital?

Wiping her mouth with the handkerchief, Goldie read the changing expressions on Florence's face and pressed in.

"You don't think that business at the hospital has anything to do with it. Do you?"

"No. No. I don't remember him saying anything about someone roaming around here in town. It was Ellis and Virginia and a missing car."

Goldie, a master manipulator, didn't hesitate.

"Virginia having one of her nervous spells again?"

"No. Don't think so. That wouldn't explain all that business about the car missing. And, for some reason, I got the feeling they were there, at the hospital, for something other than themselves."

"Oh you don't think it was Ram or Milly?"

"No. No. I'm sure they are fine. I believe Ruskin would have said something to me if it was Ram or Milly. Although I do plan to give them a call here directly. Just waiting. You know.

Until.”

“Missing car you say?”

“Ellis’s.”

Goldie and Florence sat quietly neither wanting to be the one to speak Sonny Price’s name first. They each knew how the other felt about Sonny and his people. Florence knew if it had not been for Judge and Goldalena Filbry, Sonny Price could be doing hard time or worse. He could be dead. And, Goldie knew how most people in Fulton and Tillman felt about the Prices. She also knew there were only a handful of people, her Henry for one that was there in the beginning and knew the truth. She promised Henry when they married and she promised Ollie Price on her deathbed that she would care for Sonny as her own.

Chapter Six

Ruskin entered through the emergency room doors just as the others had a few hours earlier. A wave of emotion blindsided him. There in the quiet of the stark waiting area amid scattered newspapers and mangled magazines sat Ellis Hatch in his pajamas. The hairs on his bare shins as dark and coarse as barbed wire looked like hairy socks. His eyes met Ruskin but the hangdog expression on his face meant his mind was miles away. Virginia sat next to him. Wrapped in her housecoat. Her legs crossed at the knee. Her toe tapping against the waxed, linoleum floor. She too looked up when she heard the door open but was as far away in thought as her husband. Against her chest, she held something the size of a small ham.

"Ellis? Virginia? Y'all alright?" Ruskin asked.

Ellis and Virginia sat staring off into space. Neither appeared to hear Ruskin.

"Ellis? You and Virginia doing okay this morning? Something I can help with?" Ruskin sat down opposite the couple.

"Hey Sheriff." Ellis answered as if waking from a bad dream.

Ruskin smiled and gave the two time to realize he was there to talk with them. Virginia quick to put two and two together didn't give her husband time to catch up.

"Ellis. I reckon he's here to talk to you about your car. You know. The one that has gone m-i-s-s-i-n-g!" Virginia said. Her patience worn too thin for politeness even in front of the sheriff.

Melody stirred a bit from the sudden sound of voices and Virginia snarled first at Ellis and then at Ruskin. She rocked from side to side in the hard plastic chair making shushing sounds to soothe herself and the baby. She didn't give Ruskin time to ask.

"Melody. Sonny and Kathleen's baby. Fever. But we've got the pink stuff. Should be right as rain in no time. Can't say the same for her daddy." Virginia said through a fake smile and clinched jaw.

Ruskin cleared his throat. "Well, folks." He paused making sure he didn't say kids. He almost said kids because that's what they were. Just a couple of kids. But it wasn't his place or his inclination to lecture. Not these two. It wouldn't do any good. He knew it. They knew it.

"That's what I've come to talk to you about." He said then turned his attention to Ellis avoiding Virginia's icy stare. "Ellis it's about your car."

Virginia's foot began doing double time on the floor. She adjusted herself in the chair and wrapped her arms tighter around the baby. Speaking through gritted teeth. She would feel the pain for weeks to come.

"Oh, I can tell you about that car, Sheriff. I can tell you where it was. I can tell you who was in it. But what I can't tell you and my l-o-v-i-n-g husband can't seem to find out. Is, where is the car, now? And, Sheriff don't bother telling me where you-know-who is because I'm telling you I don't care if he freezes to death."

Ellis hung his head. Ashamed. He felt the same way but would never admit it. He was glad Virginia was able to speak her mind. She was gifted that way. He just wished she would be careful about saying things she couldn't take back.

"I'm getting to that Virginia." Ruskin said. His voice dropping an octave. He had to remain calm. He couldn't let Virginia work him up in a lather. And, he couldn't risk feeling so sorry for Ellis that he allowed the situation to become personal for him. There was too much at stake to allow emotions, anyone's emotions, to hamper his investigation.

Virginia looked away to keep the tears from falling. She refused to let her anger drive her to tears. She knew she said too much. She said too much to Sonny. And, she just said too much to the sheriff. She was in over her head and didn't know how to get control.

"Ellis. Did you loan your car out to anyone last night or this morning?" Ruskin resumed.

"Sheriff, I'm not really sure." Ellis said.

"Take your time son and tell me what you are sure of."

"It was sometime after midnight, I reckon. Virginia had just about finished putting her hair up and we were getting ready to turn in when I spied Sonny cutting across the field between our two places. I know it had to have had an inch of ice on it and there he was wearing nothing but his britches. Running across there holding the baby across his arms. Dragging her blanket behind him. I reached for the door just as he cleared the porch. Virginia, she took the baby burning with fever and that's when we took off down the ridge to here. Here to the hospital. You probably heard Kathleen ain't been right since the baby. Took to bed and I reckon she's still there now. Well, we got here but it wasn't easy. The ridge is just about covered in ice and the snow had started up again. Big wet flakes falling like feathers. It sure is pretty but it ain't safe. Not if you're driving. Like I said, we got here and that's when things took off. We weren't in the door there good until Miss Semple, came out from behind them big doors over there. She took one look at the baby. Asked about the parents. And, that's when Sonny went pale. Said he couldn't go back. I took him to mean go back there behind them doors to the examination area. Guess that's how Miss Semple took it too. Because she turned tail and went through them doors like a rabbit running from buckshot. After that, we sat here for a spell and I got to noticing folks coming and going down the hall. Well, directly, I took a notion to see what was down the hall. And, when I got back, no one was here. Virginia was gone. Sonny was gone. So, I commenced to looking for them. I guess I covered most of the hospital when I decided to circle back and wait. About that time, Virginia came out from behind the big doors holding the baby and saying Sonny took off. That's it, Sheriff. That's the long and short of it. So you see. I rightly don't know just how to answer you."

Ellis sat. His elbows resting on his knees. His hands hanging between his long legs. The hair on his forearms competing with the barbed mass on his shins. He drew his face up in a quizzical expression waiting for Ruskin to impart his wisdom on the situation. Make it all right and send them on their way. Or at least to breakfast.

"Ellis. We've found your car." Ruskin started.

Ellis sat up like his name had been called at a church raffle. Virginia stopped her fidgeting and sat frozen waiting for what Ruskin had to say.

"There's been an accident. Your car went off the ridge." Ruskin waited for the news to sink in. He didn't want to finish explaining but he knew he had to say it. Say it out loud.

"Ellis, do you and Virginia know for certain, without a shadow of doubt, that it was Sonny that took your car from the hospital here this morning?" Ruskin asked hoping he was wrong.

Virginia's shoulders fell. Drawing Melody up to her chin. She bowed her head. Inhaling the sweet smell. She knew the answer was yes. Yes, it was Sonny. She saw him. Saw him leave the hospital, walk out, get in the car and drive away.

Chapter Seven

Ruskin caught glimpses of the young couple in his rearview mirror. Virginia pushing back the sea of emotion surging at the surface. Ellis searching the roadside trying to find focus. Both fighting the temptation to blame Sonny.

Driving up the ridge was dangerous even for a veteran like Sheriff Ruskin Bright. Ruts that had been cut earlier were now filled with snow. He inched slowly up the steep inclines and hugged the center of the road around each bend. Curiosity caused them all to stare down the overlook where smoke continued to rise from the burned out car and charred woods. The blood from the dead deer buried under a fresh layer of white.

Melody began to whimper and Virginia mentioned she must be hungry. Ruskin clutched the steering wheel a little tighter. Kathleen. He had to face Kathleen.

Ellis rubbed the baby's hand lying outside of the hospital blanket. Melody wrapped her tiny fingers around his and with that small gesture of affection set everything right in Ellis's forgiving heart.

Snow crunched under the car's tires as Ruskin pulled up to Sonny and Kathleen Price's small clapboard house. Theirs was the only chimney that didn't pour silver smoke. Ellis grabbed an armload of wood from the rick at the end of the porch as he made his way in behind Virginia with Sheriff Bright following close behind.

The house was dark and cold. Ellis placed the wood on the floor beside the stove. Grabbing the poker from against the wall, he pulled the door open with the end of the poker, jabbed at the handful of orange embers, and then one by one placed a few logs on them waiting and watching to see if they would take hold and begin to burn. Sheriff Bright stood just off to Ellis's side warming his hands on the slight bit of heat lifting off the stove. Ellis stood stretching out his tired back and waited for the heat.

Virginia sat on the edge of the bed with Melody still in her arms. She had hoped the sound of the door would have stirred Kathleen, or maybe the sound of footsteps in the house but that didn't do it and the weight of her on the edge of the bed didn't either.

"Guess you're gonna have to wake her Hon." Ellis said, rubbing his hands together distributing the heat now rolling out of the wood stove.

"Guess so. I just hate disturbing her." Virginia said, looking up to meet Ruskin's dark expression as he stood in the doorway separating the house's two rooms.

"Virginia why don't you lay Melody down in her bed." Ruskin said, working through a plan of readiness he had been chewing on all the way up the ridge.

Virginia nodded and complied without question. Too tired to be contrary, she was ready for someone to suggest something. Just this once, she was fine with someone telling her what to do for a change. She was ready for someone else to be in charge.

Without warning, Kathleen sat up in bed. Her hair pressed flat against her head on the right and stood out as if electrocuted on the left. Drool had dried on her chin and her hands trembled slightly then settled into her lap.

Virginia rubbed Kathleen's legs and cooed at her like a mother dove. Gently coaxing her awake. Ruskin hid his shock at Virginia's tenderness. All morning she appeared stiff with fear or dread or something unknown to him as she held the baby. But here she was, being soft. The hard edges gone.

In spite of what he was witnessing, Ruskin didn't trust it. It didn't look natural. He didn't want to believe anyone could be so cold but he had lived long enough to know the difference. Whatever Virginia's motives were, whether she knew them or not, or whether she was just going through the motions, doing what she thought was expected of her, Ruskin could see right through her. Putting on a show for those watching, was working because Kathleen was waking up and appearing to recognize everyone in the room.

Ruskin and Ellis stood as still and mute as housecats. Neither wanting to disrupt what they were seeing. Their eyes darted from Virginia to Kathleen and back to Virginia.

"Kathleen Honey, let's get you cleaned up." Virginia said, her voice soft and tender but with a slight hiss. A weak drunkard's smile broke across Kathleen's face.

"Ellis." Virginia said in a singsong way like speaking to children, "Draw up some fresh water and put a pan on the stove to warm some bath water. There should be a wash pan near the table at the back door. After that, take this slop jar out and empty it. And don't forget to rinse it." Her voice falling off at the end, "Smells like it ain't been washed in days."

Virginia turned her attention to the sheriff standing waiting for his orders. A cold chill ran down his spine. Still speaking with a lilt. "Sheriff, I don't think no one here is ready to discuss Sonny. I reckon you've got things waiting on you down the ridge."

Kathleen hearing Sonny's name repeated it under her breath. Ruskin heard it even though Virginia acted like she didn't. Virginia knew eventually Kathleen would come to her senses and realize there had been trouble seeing the sheriff standing in her house. Virginia wasn't ready to deal with it and with no more news than he had to share, she wanted the sheriff to leave before Kathleen started asking questions.

"Ahem, I'll be seeing you folks. Call if you need anything. And, do your best to stay warm and off the roads. They sure are a mess." Ruskin said feeling the need to make a show of his authority over the situation one last time. Virginia met his words with a scowl.

Ellis was making his way around from the well house with a bucket of fresh water when he saw the sheriff step off the front porch.

"Are you heading out?" Ellis asked.

"Yeah, looks like Virginia has things under control in there. I need to get back down the ridge and take another look at the car. If Sonny made it out, God only knows if he is laying hurt somewhere or." Ruskin couldn't bring himself to finish his sentence. For him, it was just too soon to be saying Sonny is dead.

Holding the water bucket Ellis said, "Let me get this water inside and if you don't mind waiting, I'll run over to the house, throw on something warm and go down there with you."

It appeared to Ruskin that Ellis had forgotten or ignored the laundry list of chores Virginia had rattled off to him. Not being one to get between and man and his wife, Ruskin lit a cigarette and waited in the warm car for Ellis.

Chapter Eight

"I stopped right about here. Pulled over to this side of the road as far as I could to leave room for any passing vehicles and walked over to where the fire truck and ambulance were parked on the opposite side of the road." Ruskin explained to Ellis pointing as he put the car in reverse, set the emergency brake with his foot and turned on the blue lights. Ellis hung on every word and detail. Glad to be dressed for the weather, he was eager to get out of the car and take a closer look.

"Well, I got to tell you Sheriff, if it'd been me coming over that rise and hitting ice sideways, I think I'd bail knowing I'd come out better with a few bumps and bruises from landing in the road than taking my chances down there." Ellis looked over the scratched guardrail rubbed black from semi-truck tires coming too close to the edge. The shortest route from Louisville to Nashville, Scots Ridge was a rite of passage for white knuckled truck drivers. One of the worse places a local could find themselves was in front of one of those big rigs burning their brakes and clutches on the downhill side of the ridge. With no shoulder to pull over and let the truck pass, most prayed for enough distance to make a sharp right hand turn onto any upcoming gravel road. The last place you wanted to end up was right where Ellis's car was now, nose down at the bottom of one of the deep ravines.

Knocking wet snow from his boots, Ruskin kicked the leaning post fastened to the bent guard rail, "so you're convinced he jumped?'

"Yep. There's no two ways 'bout it. If you say the car is empty. And I reckon that's the case. Then, that's what he done. He jumped."

"But, where?" Ruskin looked around as if to see Sonny walking up the road. Ellis turned and stepping into the slushy tracks he just left, crossed the road with no thought of any oncoming traffic. He knew the ridge like the back of his hand.

He could hear a car's engine or the shifting gears stripping on a big rig before it was in view. But Ruskin didn't trust his senses or his balance. He needed the added assurance of looking in both directions and the extra time to walk over the melting ice before crossing and following Ellis back across the road.

"What are thinking Ellis?" Ruskin took a breath and exhaled loudly waiting for Ellis to respond. "You think maybe he fell out or jumped out here? Before the car left the road?" Ruskin asked studying the way the hill just fell away from the roadside.

Ellis didn't answer. Instead he climbed over the guardrail. With his feet set sideways, he slowly descended the steep hill holding onto pine saplings and rhododendron bushes along the way.

Ruskin felt the heat of indigestion burn its way up from his stomach as his impatience grew with the whole situation. He began to wrestle with whether bringing Ellis along was a good idea. He waited at the top not sure of what Ellis was doing and was certain he had no interest in following him down the hill only to follow him back up.

Ellis got about halfway down the ravine where it leveled out for about twenty feet before dropping away again. Walking around looking at the ground and back up the side, Ellis gave Ruskin the impression he was either on to something or was trying to figure out how to make his way back up to the road.

"Find anything?" Ruskin called down the hill his hands cupped around his mouth. But there was no need for the added reinforcement, the air was so cold the sound of his voice drifted down the hill and right to Ellis's ears.

Ellis didn't answer but kept circling the small landing. Circling like a coonhound, around a tree and then looking up the tree, and then circling again. Ruskin wanted to laugh but stopped short of letting go as a car topped the rim and came over the hill slow and easy. Its tires crushing the slush almost stopping but Ruskin waved at the driver sending him politely on his way. He watched the car as it crept along and out of sight and he wondered if talk was circulating around town and folks would be finding all sorts of reasons to come up the ridge. He understood human curiosity and the strange desire to see the grotesque. But there was nothing to see here this morning, at least nothing he could see.

Ellis stood still. His back to Ruskin. Ruskin waited and tried to see or hear what Ellis was seeing or hearing. Seconds felt like minutes when the silence was once again interrupted. This time it was dispatch.

"Sheriff Bright. Calling Sheriff Bright."

"Sheriff Bright. Go ahead."

"Sheriff. It's Ivy." Ruskin shook his head. His frustration erupting nearing its crescendo. He had reminded Ivy too many times to count that she was the only dispatcher in the county and that it was not necessary to announce herself by name. But obviously, he had not reminded her enough times because once again, she had to explain in two words too many that she was on the frequency.

"Go ahead."

"Wrecker is on its way."

"Copy that."

"You on the scene?"

"We'll take it from here."

Confused, Ivy scratched her head. She didn't know who was with Sheriff Bright. Jimbo and Mac were at Patti Cake's Diner eating breakfast. She knew because her mouth was watering thinking about the hot cinnamon roll Jimbo promised to bring back to the station.

The click breaking the static on the frequency let Ivy know that the sheriff had moved on. He may be within earshot of anything further she would transmit but she also knew from her bruised pride that once she heard the click, the transmission was over. Ivy sat in the swivel chair behind the big desk at the police station entrance and watched traffic pass on Main Street. Life had come up short on many things for Ivy but she had been blessed with an infinite supply of patience. She'd wait for her cinnamon roll and she'd wait to find out just what was going on up on the ridge.

Ruskin slammed the car door sending the clap echoing

down the hollow. He returned to where he had been standing and looked down to where Ellis had been on the landing. Just as Ruskin planted his boots in the slush, he looked to find the landing empty and Ellis nowhere to be found. Nothing. No movement of any kind could be seen for as far as the trees and rising ground would allow Ruskin's tired eyes.

With the sun moving across the sky, falling heavier on the snow and ice, Ruskin knew if he didn't make a decision soon he would lose any tracks Ellis had left behind. But he had the wrecker on its way. He needed to stay put and wait on the wrecker. Running after Ellis wasn't an option. And, Ruskin feared the choice he had to make was going to cost him valuable time and information.

* * *

Ellis held his breath and his bladder. Tucked behind a thicket of briars, he watched for any movement inside the shack. How anyone could live in there was beyond his imagination. He had seen doghouses with more structural integrity. He had been inside once in all his twenty-one years. It was on a dare. The kind of dare boys make but rarely follow through on. Most boys. But he and Sonny were not most boys. They couldn't have been more than twelve. Looked more like fourteen. Fifteen when they tried. And lived harder and risked more than most twice their age.

Cutting through the woods and up the ridge he and Sonny and the Neese brothers, George, Carl, and Felix, before the three Neeses were sent to reform school later that fall, walked through Mammie Margolus's house looking for proof she was the witch everyone claimed she was and whatever else they could find. Bowed up from swearing they were the smartest, the fastest and the bravest boys in all of Jessup County, they charged into her place with no thought to what waited for them on the inside.

Now just over ten years later, Ellis Hatch squatted with-in twenty yards of the same door he and Sonny had escaped through dodging buckshot and Mammie's pack of hellhounds. The sun was pushing through the trees trying to reach the ground. Ellis had tracked someone. Someone he hoped was Sonny. Tracked them right to where he sat hunkered down and out of sight.

In a sudden burst of movement, the front door blew open spilling dogs of every color and size. Some rolling and wrestling as those behind them forcing their way out the door pushed them out into the open yard. Once outside each turned their noses up catching a scent or two or three. Frozen in place, except for their nostrils working invisible smells into their noses, they didn't appear to be an immediate threat. But, Ellis sat still desperately trying not to stir up his scent and lose control of his bladder. He watched the dogs and the door expecting at any moment Mammie would emerge or the dogs would descend. Either way, he had to be ready.

With his focus squarely on the door and the dogs, Ellis flinched with fear when he heard the hammer in the shotgun. In the matter of a split second, something secret broke in half deep within Ellis. He expected to turn around and see Sonny. See Sonny standing there with the shotgun trained on him. He expected to see Sonny too tired to out run the rumors. Sonny had lost. Lost it all. His wife. His child. His home. His mind. For the length of that one split second, Ellis was prepared to answer for everyone that had told one lie to cover another. For the first time in his life, Ellis was prepared. But as life would have it, Ellis wasn't prepared for what happened next.

"Go on get up! Get yourself up out of the bramble. I been watching you. Now go on get up to the house." Mammie Margolus used the end of the gun to make her point. The shotgun almost as long as she was tall, she held it with the expertise of a marksman. Ellis knew from experience she knew how to use it. His backside scared from the buckshot she rained down on him the last time he trespassed on her property.

Mammie marched Ellis through the pack of dogs as they sniffed at the ground where Ellis had stepped and around the hem of his pants. He stepped inside the small shack and into darkness. Following his nose to the woodstove burning hickory wood, he took the first chair he came to trusting his shin had met a solid surface that would support his weight.

The whine and crackle of the wood burning and the smell of smoked pork reminded him of how long he had been without heat and food. Hearing the door slam, a match scrapping against a hard surface and the rattle of glass, he soon saw Mammie's face shining in the halo of a coal oil lamp.

"What makes you think hiding the bushes is right?" She asked without waiting for an answer. "I been watching. Waiting for you to show up. Nobody ever teach you to knock?"

Shuffling around the little room, returning the gun to its resting place, filling two cups with steaming sassafras tea and handing one to Ellis, she sat in her rocker and watched Ellis over the rim of her cup. First one and then another of the dogs began to file inside from the back of the house.

Ellis sat quietly. This was not going as he had planned. He knew better than to get on Mammie's bad side. If she had any other side but her bad side. He knew she would turn him out leaving him with more questions than he came in with if he wasn't careful.

After their last time at her place, Sonny had bragged that she had become a friend of his. Ellis didn't believe him. He figured it was just one of Sonny's lies to make himself feel better or sound better to whoever was listening. Sonny said he had circled back the day he and Ellis and the Neese boys had been there. He had circled back and brought her a line of catfish he had caught. He never said why but that he did and that she cooked them up and they enjoyed the catfish and the best apple pie he had ever put in his mouth.

Ellis listened because that's what Ellis did. Listen. But he was never sure if Sonny was telling the truth. Over the years, Sonny would say he knew certain things were going to happen because Mammie had told him so. But, like all the times before Ellis just figured Sonny was using Mammie's name and her reputation to fill the gaps in his life. But there must have been some truth in it because Ellis had tracked Sonny right to Mammie's door. Tracked him at least to the edge of her yard. Because that's as far as he got with the tracks and his courage

Mammie sat rocking and watching. Ellis sat sipping his tea and slowly adjusting to the low light. She looked the same as she did the day he ran from her place, as if time had stood still in Pig's Eye Hollow. Her shock of hair as wiry as scrub brush. Her skin, creased and dark like a walnut. Rumor was she was the last of her gypsy bloodline. Trying to avoid her eyes, two black beads like snake eyes, he studied her hands holding her cup up to her mouth. He followed the line from her boney wrists up to her fingers gnarled with age. Their thick nicotine stained nails filed to a sharp point. The sight of this hideous crone spooked him. The whole experience reminded him of a fairy tale. Children being coaxed into the witch's house to become her supper.

Her only saving grace, the framed picture of Jesus hanging on the wall over her head. It was the same picture that hung on the wall behind the pulpit of the Tabernacle of Praise in what was the Western Auto. Hanging where he once saw tires and fan belts, he now saw Jesus every time the red light on Elm stopped him. Hers was the same picture, just smaller and in one of those frilly gold metal frames like the one his mama had of him and Virginia the day they got married. The one she had sitting on the television with the other framed pictures.

He hoped a person couldn't be a witch and have a framed picture of the Lord on the wall. She must be a good woman. At least somewhat good because on one side of the picture of the Lord was a framed picture of Frank Sinatra and on the other John Wayne. Both autographed, "To Gertie with love."

"You hungry? I reckon you got to be hungry. I've got a little fatback left over and some molasses. Can put some cabbage on if you thinking on staying a while. Hand me your cup. I'll pour you some more tea."

Mammie Margolus pushed her bent form out of the rocking chair and shuffled to the makeshift kitchen on the backside of the shack. Ellis was caught off guard by her sudden hospitality or his awareness of it. What he took for suspicion had been something else entirely. He had misunderstood her silence and stillness. She had no reason to be in a hurry. She had more answers than he had questions. She could and would wait on him to find reason to ask what she knew he had come to ask.

"Fatback and molasses sounds good. Yes Ma'am. I 'preciate the offer. Could I trouble you to point me in the direction of the outhouse?"

Mammie jerked her head in the general direction of the back of the house and left Ellis to find his way out the back door with four of the hounds as company. Stepping back out into the sharp daylight, his eyes suffering the blinding jabs deep into their sockets. Trusting the dogs would guide him to where he was going, he managed to walk out away from the house far enough to relieve his full bladder.

Standing facing the rising slope of the ridge he searched for footprints in the melting snow but found none. If Sonny had come by here, he didn't leave out this way. The dogs sensing Ellis had finished what he came to do began to turn back toward the house and its warmth. Satisfied he had tracked Sonny this far and that Mammie could answer to Sonny's whereabouts, he followed the dogs back inside.

"You ever heard the story about how this holler came to be called Pig's Eye?" Mammie handed Ellis a plate with a black puddle of molasses and four strips of fatback floating on top. Returning to where he had been sitting, he crossed his leg placing his foot on his knee and balanced the tea on the side of his boot like he had seen his daddy do so many times before freeing up his hands to dredge the pork through the sticky goodness. His polite silence gave way to her story whether he had heard it before or not.

"Nah, I reckon a boy your size and age has probably heard it a time or two." She paused giving Ellis time to ask what he came to ask. Everyone that made it as far as inside her house came for one reason or another but they always came full of questions needing answers. It felt to Ellis like she could see right through him.

Ellis stopped chewing. The cup resting on his foot tipped forward almost spilling tea. He reached for it just in time fearing he would use up his precious time saying how sorry he was for spilling tea all over the yellow newspaper covering her floor. He managed a polite nod believing she already knew why he had shown up at her place unannounced and believing if he tried to speak his tongue had forgotten how to move.

Without a preamble, Mammie told how she could smell fear rushing down the hollow long before she heard Sonny's familiar footfall and his frantic knock on her door before sunrise. She told how she made his favorite. Fatback, molasses and sassafras tea. She told how he practically swallowed it whole leaving only the few pieces that Ellis had enjoyed. She said she asked about Kathleen and the baby and that's where she stopped. Careful not to breach a confidence, she pulled back the veil only slightly allowing Ellis to fill in the missing pieces. The last thing she shared was the advice she gave Sonny. She told him to take stock.

Respectfully, Ellis let her words sink in and take root. He believed Sonny would have done whatever the old woman said. He believed Sonny probably did go home. Stayed home long enough to take stock but didn't stay. Ellis didn't want to disagree with Mammie. He knew she meant well.

"You go about your way. It'll take time. He'll find his way."

Looking at the floor, too overcome by the weight of her words and wisdom. Ellis asked, "But how do you know? How can you..."

"How can I what? Be certain?" She asked.

Turning his face up to meet her eyes. The crow's feet fanning out from the corners of her eyes like rays of sunlight on a child's drawing. Her mouth turned up in a gentle smile exposing her toothless hard gums.

"It's the ways of man."

Ellis looked into her eyes, then up into the eyes of Jesus, then Sinatra and then the Duke. He thought if he looked into his own he might see the same assurance reflecting back at him. But then again, probably not.

Chapter Nine

The morning hours had burned off carrying with them the threatening clouds. Peeled back and exposed, the midday sky with its fixed crown of sunshine lifted the day's temperature and melted the snow and ice. Winter birds sang praise anthems and all of nature responded. Within minutes of stores opening for the day's business, cars lined Tillman's town square like dominoes. People from all over Jessup County were milling about ticking off their Saturday morning chore lists.

Deep in Pig's Eye Hollow Sonny Price sat on a jutted slab of limestone weighing his options. The blisters on his feet had ballooned to the size of silver dollars. His pants soaked to the knees. He couldn't remember the last time he was this cold and exhausted. He feared his left shoulder was out of socket because he couldn't raise his arm. He ran his hand over the goose egg on the left side of his forehead and knew his eyes had to be black from such a hard blow to the head.

Lighting a Marlboro red he chuckled thinking about the condition he was in and how his cigarette lighter survived the fall from the car without a scratch. That was just his luck. He looked and felt like he had been beaten to a pulp and the one thing he had that belonged to his daddy, Tinkum's Zippo lighter, looked brand new.

Inhaling the warm cigarette smoke, Sonny thought back over the night and morning. His mind ran from one end of the county to the other and one extreme to the other. So did his anger. He was doling out judgment and wasn't leaving anyone out.

He was angry with Mammie. For the first time in his life, he was angry with the one person he had confided in since he was twelve years old. She knew everything. But that didn't stop him from being angry with her. After telling her, once again, how he couldn't find a way to live up to everyone's expectations, all she could offer was one of her crazy gypsy riddles.

Take stock. That's what she told him. Shaking his head, Sonny dislodged Mammie from his mind.

He was angry with Mud Flats. That stinking strip of earth he called home. Four warped walls and a rusted roof attached to a porch that tipped south, situated on a plot of land he couldn't even call his own, made him fighting mad just to think about it. Regardless of Kathleen's current emotional state, he had to rid his mind of that place.

Kathleen. He was angry with her too. He admitted it. Admitted it to Mammie and admitted it to himself. He should feel ashamed but he didn't. There was just too much anger.

Then there were all the others. The ones that sold him out. Acted like they cared about him but the minute things turned ugly, they betrayed him just like he suspected eventually they would. He should have been surprised. He wanted to be surprised. But, he knew Ellis wasn't going to keep turning the other cheek. When he saw Ellis and Virginia pull up to the house with Sheriff Bright, he knew then it was time to get gone and be gone for good.

How they didn't know he was right there standing just outside the back door was no longer a concern of his. He had trudged up the ridge, through the woods from Pig's Eye where he left the car to burn out, and up the rise to Mud Flats. Kathleen didn't stir when he came in rustling around their bedroom opening one dresser drawer after another finding a shirt and socks. She didn't even turn over when he almost knocked over the chamber pot under the foot of the bed trying to find his boots. He thought he heard her say his name when he opened the back door fighting the knob and his coat with his injured arm. He had just managed to get the door latched when he heard their voices. Virginia calling the shots and Ellis falling into step. He had just made it to the tree line when he saw the sheriff's car roll out of sight and Ellis sitting on the passenger side.

There was nothing left there for him. No one would be sitting up this time waiting for him to come home. He knew how to leave. He had done it before. Pulling the last drag from the cigarette, he belched from the fatback that had turned on him too. Studying the sky and the wet ground, he eased off the rock and headed deeper into the hollow.

* * *

Ruskin stood on the side of the road as the wrecker backed up against the guardrail for support. Its yellow lights danced in the sunlight bouncing off the dark wet bark of the pines and cedars. Jimbo got out of the wrecker on the passenger side and Mac pulled the deputy's car up behind Ruskin's.

"What a night." Mac said crossing the road to where Ruskin stood looking down the hill at the mechanic and deputy working to harness the car and extract it from its fiery grave.

"Yep, it's been a long one. You boys see Ellis Hatch on your way up here? He was here with me but took off down through the woods. Thought maybe he worked his way back up to the road and was on his way back up here." Ruskin asked studying the work going on at the bottom of the hill.

"Nah, Sir, can't say we did. That Ellis Hatch is a good one. Helps Sonny get the baby to the hospital, loses his car, and then they both go missing."

"Right now, we can only confirm one missing person. Sonny Price. Let's keep our facts straight and not go off on some wild goose chase. Ellis is about. He's probably home by now."

"Yes, Sir Sheriff. Sure is a mess though. Don't you think?"

Ruskin returned to his car parked on the opposite shoulder giving room to allow the wrecker to lift the burned out car through the opening in the guardrail and onto the road. He needed to steer clear of any speculation and his young deputies like most of the people in the county would be forming opinions of what had happened overnight. Ruskin was just as human as the rest of them and could form his own opinion. He had to stay focused. He had to find Sonny and pray Ellis was where he belonged. Safe at home.

"Sheriff, I can run this over to the junk yard or keep it at the shop. Whatever works for you?" Elrod Bishop, Jimbo's brother and wrecker service and mechanic for the county said getting back in the cab of the wrecker. Jimbo climbed back in on the passenger side and adjusted the heater.

"Thank ya Elrod. Why don't you and Jimbo take it on over to the shop. We'll keep it there until we know what Ellis wants to do with it. It'll give us time to take one more look through her before she gets out of our hands."

"You got it Sheriff. We'll see you boys in town." Elrod tipped his cap to Ruskin and Mac and slowly pulled away from the guardrail and out onto the road.

"Mac you go ahead and make your rounds this morning paying close attention to any damage the weather may have caused overnight and radio in anything you may see. If you happen upon Sonny Price or Ellis Hatch pick them up. Unofficially. They are not being arrested. Just brought in for questioning and safety. Understand?"

"Yes, Sir, Sheriff. See you back at the station." Mac drove off without a second look.

Ruskin decided to take the time and return to Ellis and Virginia's to see if Ellis had returned home. If so, he wanted an explanation and he thought maybe he owed the boy an apology. He wasn't sure why he felt that way but saying I'm sorry never injured anyone.

A ribbon of silver smoke curled from Sonny and Kathleen's chimney. Although the house didn't look any cheerier from the outside, the chimney gave the impression things were improving on the inside. Its light yellow paint had faded to a pale cream and the eaves and windowsills dripped from the melted snow and ice as if shedding tears from all they had witnessed.

Ruskin tapped his horn twice announcing his arrival before approaching the house. With no one coming to the door, he stomped across the front yard, keeping the mud from collecting on his boots and to make as much noise as necessary to come near the house. Still no one came to the door so he scraped the wet from his boots on the porch steps and called out to anyone inside. Still no movement from within. Knowing this wasn't unusual with sickness inside he still felt uneasy with no one coming to the door or at least moving to the window to look out and motion for him to come ahead.

With the customary approach to the house out of the way, Ruskin knocked on the door with three hard raps and called out to anyone inside. Looking back out across the yard he began to doubt if anyone was inside. There had been enough strangeness overnight that he was beginning to believe anything was possible with this bunch of escape artists. Sonny leaves the hospital. Nowhere to be found. Ellis disappears in the woods. Without a trace. And, now Virginia. And Kathleen. And the baby.

Just then Ruskin heard the baby cry. Someone was inside. He rapped on the door again. Three solid knocks and called out to Virginia.

"Virginia! It's Ruskin. Sheriff Bright. Y'all okay in there?"

The door inched open and Kathleen stood holding the baby.

"Morning Kathleen."

"Come on in, Sheriff. Forget something?"

"Pardon me?" Ruskin stepped just inside the front door. Looking around he could see a bottle warming in a pan of water on the wood stove. And, just around the door separating the living room and the bedroom, he could see Virginia's bare feet hanging off the side of the bed. She was on her side and as the room fell quiet, he could hear the soft rhythmic sound of a woman snoring.

"When you were here earlier. When you brought Ellis and Virginia home. By the way, has Ellis figured out what's wrong with his car? I know we all depend on it now that Sonny can't get the radiator in our old clunker any time soon." Kathleen smiled, it was weak but she managed a smile. Shaking the bottle of milk to warm it through, she shook out a few drops on the underside of her wrist while holding the baby still swaddled in the hospital blanket. She walked slowly almost tiptoeing to the rocking chair by the wood stove and began feeding the baby. She nodded for Ruskin to help himself to one of the other chairs in the room while she rocked and fed the baby.

Ruskin eased himself down into a chair across the room where he could see Kathleen fully and where Virginia could see him if she should wake while he was there. He had no idea how long his visit would be because he was surmising the scene as it played out.

Just two hours earlier, Kathleen was woken to a house full and her husband nowhere among the group. Now, she sits in her small living room, washed and dressed in a pretty shirtwaist, her hair combed and twisted in bun and her baby wrapped in the stolen blanket only hours earlier to protect her from the fierce weather as she made her way back home. Ruskin looked around the room for the small bottle of pink antibiotic the doctor had given Virginia but it was nowhere in sight. His ribcage swelled as he inhaled deeply trying to steady his reaction. He was just as upset with himself as he was with the circumstances. He expected too much from everyone and he had only himself to blame for the constant disappointment that smacked him in the face when folks didn't met those expectations and let him down.

He expected Sonny and Kathleen to be more responsible before bringing a baby into their marriage. Sonny was fully equipped and able to get this house in full repair before adding another to it. He had all the advantages if not more than Ellis with so many being willing to give the boy all he needed and wanted.

Ruskin's mind shifted to Ellis and Virginia. Both making the most of their circumstances. Working hard to make a home of the house across the tobacco field, they had not filled it yet with the children everyone hoped and prayed for but they were open to helping Sonny and Kathleen with Melody. And poor Melody, a little lost lamb in all this. Sick with a fever and needing her mama's attention came out on the short end of the stick with these four.

"Whew, Kathleen I think I could sleep for a week and not feel as rested as I did with those few minutes." Virginia was pressing her hair in place still in pin curls tied up with a floral headscarf. She stopped short of coming in to the living room when she saw Ruskin sitting in the chair opposite Kathleen as she burped the baby. Kathleen smiled and Ruskin looked frozen stiff like the mannequins in the window at Newberry's on the Square.

"Sheriff Bright. What brings you back out here two times in one morning?" Virginia busied herself around the living room filling a wash pan with dried beans. Ruskin timed his answer to each handful of beans she tossed in the metal pan with a slap.

"Just checking on y'all. Making sure you don't need anything before I head back to town."

"Why Sheriff you make it sound like we are new to this. Me and Kathleen are old pros when it comes to fending for ourselves. Who do you think manages things around here when them boys you call men decide to spend all night coon hunting or frog gigging or whatever it is that keeps them going to the Red Stagg?" Virginia snarled, separating the tiny pieces of gravel from the beans.

Ruskin shook his head not knowing what to say. He didn't want to lock horns with Virginia Hatch. Her tongue was as sharp as his boning knife and just as precise. He figured despite her proclamation of a good nap, she was wrung out from all that had been placed in her lap and the venom she was spewing had been backed up for a while. He was not its intended target. That he knew for certain.

"I'm going to put these beans on and make a fresh pot of coffee. You're welcome to stay. For the coffee, the beans won't be done for hours." Virginia's snarl broke into a toothy grin as disturbing a possum caught in headlights. Her tone sent the message loud and clear. Ruskin was over staying his welcome.

"No, no coffee for me. Like I said, I was making my way back down the ridge and just wanted to stop in before getting back to town." He looked around the room once more before crossing to the door and opening it. The rush of cold air caused him to close it but not latch it letting the women know he was just as good out on the porch but didn't want to usher in the cold weather and let the heat escape. Suddenly he felt akin to

Sonny and Ellis and envied their absence.

Wiping her hands on the cup towel draped over her lap, Virginia placed the pan of beans in the chair and said she would walk the sheriff outside and toss the bean gravel out into the yard. Kathleen was still busy trying to get the baby to burp and didn't think twice of the sheriff's visit or Virginia's excuse to toss the bean gravel in the yard instead of back in the beanbag as usual.

"What's going on, Sheriff? I'm not buying this welcome wagon story." Virginia said, she planted her feet squaring off to brace herself against his answer and the cold wind rushing up her housecoat.

"It's Ellis. Thought he might have circled back around and came home."

"Ellis! He didn't come back with you?"

"No."

Ruskin now braced himself for the tongue-lashing that appeared to be rising up from deep within Virginia. It's rumbling and tumbling rolling up her body in waves.

"Don't worry about Ellis Hatch, Sheriff Bright. He knows his way home."

Ruskin was bowled over by her sudden change in tone and attitude. In one minute she was ranting about being left to her own devices in the absence of her husband and in the next she was defending his wandering ways.

Not sure exactly what the appropriate response was, Ruskin politely said good bye and walked to his car feeling the heat of Virginia's eyes boring holes in his back. If she knew anything about Ellis's whereabouts or for Sonny's for that matter, she would go to her grave with the information. Ruskin would have to find other ways to get the information he needed to find the missing men. Praying against all hope it was only one missing man or that they would be found together.

Chapter Ten

Whirling tornadoes of red dirt danced down rows of leafy tobacco and corn. Waist high to most men the green crops looked to yield a healthy return. Sonny daydreamed about days he and Ellis worked the fields around and between their two houses. Land that had been passed down from generation to generation plowed by mule and more recently by tractor. With Sonny gone, Ellis would be left to work the fields alone. Squatting in the shadows of the tree line, just out of sight of Kathleen hanging laundry on the clothesline, Sonny lined up between rows of corn and watched his wife and daughter.

Almost seven months old, Melody sat on the quilt pallet gnawing on her rattle. The sound of the beads scraping inside the plastic toy sailed down the row when the wind picked up. Sonny appreciated the late afternoon breezes. Breezes that lifted his spirits and his wife's skirt tail affording him an occasional glimpse of her thighs. Kathleen laughed as she hung sheets on the line playing peek-a-boo with the baby. Sonny laughed too. He wanted to rush out of his hiding place. Rush down the field between rows of green and into the backyard of his home. Into the arms of his family.

Months spent in the deepest parts of Pig's Eye Hollow, sleeping in a truck bed of Arvis Ange's junkyard. His only means of shelter, the truck topper. His only means of comfort, three flea bitten bird dogs. In the beginning, he had every intention to go home. He even counted the days. Numbering them as if to arrive at some magical number on a specific date to go home. But, that day had not arrived and he had long since stopped counting.

Days spent doing odd jobs around the junkyard repaying Arvis for his room and board. His room, a rusted out '36 Ford with its makeshift topper of splintered plywood and threadbare-tarred canvas. His board, a helping of what got tossed out to the dogs or whatever could be slapped between two slices of light bread. The choice of meals was a decision he made after seeing rats as large as cats running in and out from under Arvis Ange's house. If he had to choose, Sonny decided he'd eat with the dogs. If he was going to get bit over a meal. He'd rather it be a dog bite.

Arvis peddled around the county bartering and wheeling and dealing with anyone wanting to do business. It had been rumored as long as anyone could remember that he was the richest man in Jessup County. Jilted by the love of his life before he was old enough to shave, Arvis settled in at his home place, the bottomland of deepest hollow in the county, and created a life and world of his own. Like the Greek gypsy woman, his nearest neighbor by three miles as the crow flies, anyone deciding on visiting him had to have been born with an extra measure of courage or a deep abiding faith in the Almighty. Arvis wasn't sure which Sonny Price had but he had known the boy since he made his appearance in this world. He owed it to Tinkum Price and the sisters to take care of the boy as best he could. It was his turn to do his part.

Sonny worked his way through the mixed match collection of rusting engine parts and broken appliances scattered about the side yard. He was whistling the tune he had heard Kathleen singing to Melody. Something she had heard on the radio. Returning to the bucket of catfish he had been cleaning before he took off to ease his mind and curiosity of Kathleen. He didn't see Arvis standing behind the screen door watching him. Studying him.

Letting the door slam behind him Arvis started in with one of his many lectures. "You get done with those catfish let me know. I've got a carburetor that needs bleeding and by the looks of your hands. You are well on your way."

"Can't tell the difference right now. Not sure if this is fish blood or mine. Whiskers cut like razors."

"Son you act like you ain't never had a'body show you nothing."

Sonny winced. Words cutting deeper than the catfish whiskers. He hated taking grief off of the old man but had no choice. He couldn't go home. From what Arvis had said from talk in town, Sonny was presumed dead. How they could decide on his death when there wasn't a body to confirm such a story was distinction without a difference as far as Arvis was concerned. Sonny had come to accept it. He was gone and the town including Kathleen had moved on. Proving what he believed all along, the world could go right on spinning without him in it.

* * *

Goldie Filbry sat in Chilton's filing station's metal folding chairs inhaling exhaust fumes and cursing under her breath upset with waiting on her car.

"Junior, you told me an hour ago that my car would be ready. Now, I want to talk to your daddy. He is here isn't he? Man owns a business for twenty-five years and leaves his half-wit son in charge needs to have his own brain checked out." Goldie said, adjusting the collar of one of her husband's summer shirts.

"Mrs. Filbry, I'm standing right here and can hear every word you're saying," Junior said, his face burning from her insult, "and yes, Pop is here somewhere but I don't need to go get him to answer your questions about your car. Now, I told you just a few minutes ago...hey there Mrs. Eubanks 'preciate the business. Y'all let us know if those brakes start squeaking again and we'll take a look."

"Prissy, I'd take it on down the road to Elrod's garage if you start having trouble again. You could find yourself like me with your car up on that doohickey with nobody in the place here to tell you why it's up in the rafters and nobody with the sense of a frog to get it down. I came in for an oil change and I'm still sitting here." Goldie said waving at the white haired woman wrestling her coin purse back into her purse.

"Now Mrs. Filbry that ain't nice telling Mrs. Eubanks that. You know you'd catch more flies with honey..."

"Junior, I'm not here to catch flies. I'm here to get my Buick. That one right there up on that thing-a-ma-gig y'all got it hoisted up on. I don't see how in the world it can take a body as long as it takes you to do what needs to be done. Get in there and get it fixed or get it down and let me take it down the road. I'm sure there's someone in Nashville or any place between here and there that can figure out what's going on with it. I've got places to go. I can't be about this place all day." Goldie said, twisting the chain of her husband's pocket watch around her finger. Junior eyeballing the watch and her ill-fitting clothes.

"It's like I told you Mrs. Filbry. We've got to wait on the part. Should be here any minute. We get that new part on there and you're good to go." Junior explained then dismissed the old woman to ring up another customer ready to get his car back on the road.

Goldalena Filbry didn't budge from the counter helping herself to the bag of peanuts sitting near the cash register. Running her thumbnail down the center seam, she opened the shell, tossed the two boiled nuts into her mouth and then stacked the shells into a pile on the counter.

"Here you go Mrs. Filbry. Help yourself. That's what they're there for." Junior smiled, scooting the peanuts and another small brown paper bag with its top rolled down like a shirtsleeve. "You can put the shells in here."

Goldie peered over into the bag as Junior tilted it for her to look in and see the bottom covered in discarded shells.

"Junior? I'm going to pull up here and get some water for the radiator if that'll be alright?" Ben Hardy said looking to the young man his face covered in pimples and beads of sweat both caused by an anxious disposition.

"Yes Sir Mr. Hardy. Help yourself. Let me know if you need anything else."

"I wouldn't do that if I were you Ben." Goldie said spitting bits of peanut.

"What's that?" Ben said realizing he had walked into an unpleasant situation. "How you doing Goldalena? How's your bunions? Those foot pads helping?" Ben smiled trying to diffuse the tension or draw it off the boy.

"My feet are just fine thank you very much and it is a

good thing 'cause I reckon I'll have to walk to town from here on out if these nitwits can't figure out how to get my Buick out of the air."

"Well, these boys seem to know what they're doing." Ben said smiling at Junior. Junior's ears, like two open car doors on either side of his lemon shaped head, flushed red. His thin lips slid back off his yellow teeth.

"Let's you and me walk out here and leave them to it." Ben said opening the door for Goldie to pass in front of him.

"I know what you're doing Benjamin Hardy. You ain't fooling no one." Goldie said as she stepped out into the noonday sun.

The service station door closed behind them with soft rattle of the bell. Goldie cut her eyes to the side to see Junior still standing behind the counter watching as she and Ben made their way over to where his panel truck was parked at the pumps. She motioned with her hand for the boy to get on with his work but he just stood there staring.

"I ain't never in all my life seen anyone so confounded slow as that boy. How in the world he manages to get his pants on straight in the morning is beyond me." Goldie said pulling up her dead husband's pants around her thick waist.

"Don't reckon me or you either one needs to fret over whether he knows how to do anything but what he is told. And, I'm guessing he has been told to manage that counter. The boy knows figures like you know your name. It's a waste of talent and God's gift that he is even in that station doing anything. A mind like his. He ought to be in Nashville at one of the universities studying medicine or engineering. Why he is as smart as any of them space boys in Houston they keep talking about in the papers." Ben said as he poured water into his truck's radiator.

Goldie choked on a peanut hull laughing, "Can you just imagine that boy a rocket scientist? Oh yeah, I can see him getting a rocket in the air. I just can't see him getting one down." Ben laughed too but not at Junior, at his old classmate, Goldalena Filbry. Her bad temper was second only to her dry sense of humor. If she was cracking jokes, then she was cooling off and that was best for everyone.

"So tell me. What are you doing here anyway? That's you're Buick up there on the rack?" Ben risked asking on the heels of her joke as he put the water can back under the hydrant.

Goldie handed him a shop towel that had been left on the pump for him to wipe his hands. "Yeah, that's mine. Been up there half the morning. Something about the brakes. Had to send out to get a part. Brought it in for the oil change and they get to monkeying around and tell me the brakes need work." She said.

"Well now Goldalena, you don't need to be running around town with bad brakes. One trip down the ridge and you'll be like that Price boy. Gone." Ben said, closing the truck hood with a slam. He had called her by her birth name. For Goldie, that was a term of endearment by a handful of people that could stop her in her tracks and sway her opinion.

"Pssh, that Price boy took off on his own volition. I don't care what they say. No body found means there's still a body to be found. And I don't rightly appreciate you comparing me to yet another bone headed man in town." Goldie said regretting the words before they left her mouth. She had never spoke against Sonny Price but her patience was spent.

"No one is comparing anyone here. I just don't want to hear you've gone off the ridge because you were too impatient to get your brakes properly repaired. That's all I'm saying." Ben said coaxing a smile from her.

"All I know is I've got places to be and ain't getting nowhere fast."

"Here, take my truck. I've done made my rounds today. Everyone has been seen about. You go ahead. Do what it is that's got you pressed for time and I'll wait on your car. When you're done come by the house. Me and the Buick and your new brakes will be there waiting on you."

"Well you don't have to tell me twice." Goldie said snatching the keys from his hands. Ben watched as his truck with its faded red "Hardy Goods" sign disappeared down the street. He could hear the gears grind as she found them and feared he would be back in the service station before the week was out needing a new clutch. No deed goes unpunished he reminded himself and turned to wait inside the air-conditioned service station for the Buick.

Chapter Eleven

Goldie tapped on the panel truck's horn. The blaring noise could wake the dead bringing Florence Bright to her front door wondering if it was the Second Coming. Mumbling under her breath, filled with frustration from spending too much time at the service station and fighting the truck's steering wheel, Goldie killed the engine. The truck backfired jerking the poor widow forward and sending a cloud of oily smoke down the driveway and across the street to her yard.

"Come on in Goldie." Florence shouted over the hissing and popping of the truck's engine cooling as she leaned out her front door. Her hands dripping with soap suds. She did her best to hide her shock seeing her neighbor driving Mr. Hardy's roaming store truck. The old woman never ceased to amaze Florence.

"Come to get you Florence Bright. Dry your hands and get your shoes on."

"I've got too much to get done around here today to go to town."

"We ain't going to town. Well at least not that I know of."

"What? Won't you get out of that truck? What you doing in that old thing anyway? Come on in where it's cool. You got to be burning up riding in that truck. Come on inside and have something cold to drink." Florence said, stepping barefooted across her front yard knowing all the while Ruskin would have a fit if he knew she was walking in the grass instead of the sidewalk. But, what Ruskin didn't know wouldn't hurt him, and the hot sidewalk would hurt Florence's bare feet.

With Goldie following behind her through the front door, Florence kept right on talking. "You feeling alright? Got one of your headaches? I think I might have some headache powders. Ruskin may have taken the last one. Let me go check. Bless his heart between keeping those boys he calls deputies reined in and dealing with that silly Ivy Moore, it's a wonder

Ruskin's head don't just snap off. I'll be right back with those powders."

Exasperated, Goldie exhaled loudly as she plopped down too hard onto one of the four vinyl covered kitchen chairs. Her soft flesh recoiled under her husband's sweat soaked summer shirt sending ripples up her torso. "I ain't needing no headache powders. Sit. Sit down and listen." Florence eased down in the kitchen chair opposite Goldie. The damp cup towel hanging over her shoulder made a wet patch on her white cotton sleeveless top exposing her white cotton bra strap.

Florence sat patiently letting Goldie collect her thoughts and her composure. Whatever had her this riled up was worth the wait. She hoped she wouldn't have to ask why Goldie was driving Mr. Hardy's roaming store truck. Surely that mystery would be revealed soon enough. Secretly, Florence had been hoping Goldie would accept Ben Hardy as a suitor. Maybe that was why Goldie's face flushed and her breath short. But then again, it could be the weather and trying to handle the panel truck.

"I saw him!" Goldie managed three words and waited for Florence to catch up.

"Him? You saw him? You've got to give me more than that to go on. Here let's have us some lemonade and give you time to settle in a bit. Driving Mr. Hardy's truck has got you wore out." Florence was hoping mentioning the truck would shift the conversation in that direction. She was more interested in the truck and less about gossiping about someone Goldie saw or thought she saw. If she didn't get her to talking about the truck and Mr. Hardy, Goldie would get fixated on this other man and never get back to why she was driving the truck.

"Hmmm, lemonade." Goldie said smacking her tongue and lips realizing how parched she actually was.

"Lemonade sounds good but don't you mind fixing none. I've got a pitcher already made over at my house. Give me a minute and I'll be right back with it in hand."

Goldie started to get up, wobbled a bit, and sat down again just as hard as the first time. Her eyes the size of saucers.

She had overheated or was too excited or a combination of both. Either way, she needed to sit down and stay put.

"Please sit. Sit. I'll go get the lemonade!" Florence pleaded. The last thing she needed was to have her neighbor fall out from heat or excitement on her just-mopped-and-waxed kitchen floor, especially since she has yet to utter one word of anything interesting!

"Okay, here we go. Now, we both have a nice glass of your lemonade. Best stuff in all of Jessup County. So you were saying something about seeing someone while you were out in Mr. Hardy's truck?" Florence coaxed as she caught her breath from sprinting across the street remembering to put on her shoes before leaving her house to keep from scalding her bare feet on the asphalt street and then to remember to remove her shoes before going inside the Filbry's and then to remember to do it all again in reverse.

Goldie eyed Florence from over the Tupperware tumbler the ice rushing down to meet her dry lips. The lemonade had once again done its magic. She knew Florence was anxious to hear why she was in Ben Hardy's roaming store panel truck. But, Florence would have to wait. First things first and Goldie didn't jostle her guts for four miles bouncing on the driver's seat of that rattle trap Ben Hardy passed off as a means of transportation to be rushed through a conversation as important as this. No, Florence will just have to wait this one out.

"I said, I saw him. Took me long enough but I knew if I waited I would soon find the thief that ran off with my Henry's coveralls!" Goldie announced with pride pushing her orange plastic tumbler across the table for a refill.

Florence poured her more lemonade and prayed it would not run out before her patience did.

"Henry's coveralls?" Florence asked shaking her head trying her best to remember if she knew anything about a missing pair of coveralls.

"Yes. Yes. Henry's coveralls. The same coveralls that went missing about six, oh maybe, seven months ago. The same coveralls," Goldie took a sip of lemonade, "that took legs and ran off the same time I saw someone run out from my cellar!"

Both women remembered the night in question but not the same way. Florence vaguely remembered her neighbor saying something about her cellar. About hearing the cellar door or something about the cellar door. Was it that it was unlocked? Was it left opened? She knew she didn't remember anything about missing coveralls or someone being in the cellar. There was so much going on that night with Sonny Price. It was then that Florence realized it had been several months since she even thought about Sonny Price and that Ruskin hadn't said a word. She wondered if Ruskin had called off the investigation. She wondered if the search for Sonny or his body was over.

Goldie regretted saying anything when she saw the look on Florence's face. She knew she had not shared everything that night. She couldn't share everything then because she had to do whatever it took to protect Sonny. If it was Sonny in her cellar, she needed to know. But, as weeks turned into months and not hide nor hair of the boy to be seen of or heard of, she figured if it was him, then she would let the coveralls go. It wasn't until today that she knew for certain it wasn't Sonny Price that took the coveralls.

Florence wiped her face with the damp towel before asking what she feared.

"Are you saying you saw the man who was in your cellar that night? You saw him, today?"

Gone was the curiosity of the panel truck. Whatever the reason was that Goldalena Filbry was driving around in Ben Hardy's panel truck, couldn't be nearly as interesting as who this mystery man is and where she saw him.

"That's what I'm saying Florence." Goldie said with a confessional tone.

Both women sat quietly sipping on their lemonade letting the thoughts and images settle on their minds. The phone rang startling them both out of their stupor.

Florence moved as if in slow motion to the ringing phone. Answered. Said two words. And then, slowly came back to the table. Goldie's eyebrows asked the question. Florence responded, "Wrong number."

"So, you saw the person that broke into your cellar back in the winter and stole Judge Filbry's coveralls? You saw him today?" Florence asked.

"Yes. That's what I'm saying."

Relaxing back in her chair, Florence placed her hands in her lap and listened as Goldie explained.

"I took my Buick in for its regular oil change this morning. I've been trading at Chilton's for as long as I can remember. He does good work and I trust him. Henry trusted him. And, I do too. I had settled in to one of those folding chairs they have sitting just inside the office area. Not much of an office, I reckon, although there is that little space there behind the counter where Dorothy keeps the books. I was sitting there waiting and visiting with first one then another when I happen to see a man shuffle around inside the garage. Out there where they had my Buick up on the rack, I think that's what they call it. Anyways, I kept watching and studying on this man. I had never seen him before but there was something sort of familiar about him. Well, I didn't want to be peculiar about it so I tried not to stare but I'm telling you every chance I got to look out the glass in the door into the service area, I did trying to catch a better look of this fellar. I guess I could have said something but the longer I studied on it the less I knew just what to say. And, well, like I said, I was visiting with first one then another and got distracted every time I thought I had figured out some way of asking about the man. Directly, I took the notion to stand up at the counter and visit with Junior. Figuring I'd catch a better look if I was standing right there in the door so to speak. I wasn't up at the counter no time until Junior takes off out in the service area leaving me standing there chewing on air and peanuts. They have boiled peanuts at the counter. I helped myself. Well, I reckon Junior must have thought I was in a hurry about the Buick 'cause he came a high tailing inside and rambling on about my brakes needing fixing and how there was some part that needed to be replaced and how he had sent the man to fetch it. I guess that's when it happened because I wasn't prepared to hear my Buick needed any additional work and I sure as heck didn't expect to hear that the fellar wearing Henry's coveralls was the one that had gone to fetch the part. Well, I got a bit flustered with all this information coming at me so sudden like and considering I needed answers and I needed my Buick, I probably let in to the boy a little too hard and well..."

Goldie rattled the melting ice in her Tupperware glass and drank the last sip of watered down lemonade. Florence poured a half of a glass making sure to leave some in the pitcher not knowing where this story was going and how long it was going to take to get there.

"...Ben showed up. Offered for me to take his truck. Offered for me to use it today and then meet him at his house this evening to switch it out for my Buick."

Florence felt deflated. She waited. Waited to hear the rest. There had to be more.

Goldie reached for the pitcher of lemonade. Poured off the rest topping off her glass and Florence's.

"So, that's what I'm saying. We need to go find out what we can about this man. Get your shoes and let's go."

"But wait a minute Goldie. If you said he has gone to get a part for your car, shouldn't we just go back over to Chilton's and wait for him to come back. You can talk to him then."

Florence couldn't believe what she was saying. She was suggesting they confront this stranger. She was suggesting they drive over to Chilton's Service Station in Ben Hardy's panel truck and ask a complete stranger why he was wearing Judge Henry Filbry's coveralls. Coveralls that he stole six months ago from the judge's cellar.

Goldie shook her head with every word that Florence said. "No. That won't work."

Florence's shoulders fell in relief that her suggestion wasn't the right answer. She wasn't excited about figuring out how to backpedal her way out of that one.

"We are going to see Della"

"Della? Della Cross? What's she got to do with this?"

"Sturgill and Della's place is the closet one to Raymond and Dorothy Chilton's farm. If anyone is going to know what is going on at the filling station or up on the hill at the farm, it's going to be Della."

"But how do you know she is even going to be home? She could be out doing something. Does she even know we are heading that way?"

"They're working on their stamp books."

"Who is?"

"Della and her sisters. Travis, Kitty's husband, Della's sister, I think she is the third one, maybe she is one of the twins, I can't keep that bunch straight, anyway, Travis was in getting a fan belt at Chilton's and I heard him say they were all over at Della's filling their stamp books. So, we are as good as gold when it comes to finding out who this man is with my Henry's coveralls and anything else we might be in the need for knowing."

Chapter Twelve

The panel truck backfired. A plume of oily black smoke blossomed from its backside and poured forward reaching the truck's cab just as Goldie and Florence opened their doors. Goldie's dentures were still rattling making her look and sound like she was shivering with cold in spite of the warm weather. Florence expected a bumpy ride after seeing the condition Goldie was in just an hour earlier when she showed up at her place but nothing could have prepared her for the four mile gut jerking drive.

Still feeling the truck's vibrating cab, Florence's legs trembled as she followed Goldie to Della's front porch. Her heels bouncing but never touching the ground. Her knees in a perpetual bend keeping time with her heels. And her elbows bent at her waist, flapping like chicken wings from the truck's poor suspension, made her look like she was doing some strange dance. She would have been extremely embarrassed had it not been that Goldie was doing the same jig two strides ahead of her.

Waiting for someone to come to the door, Florence realized her teeth were chattering too. Fearing she would bite her tongue if she attempted to say anything she decided to plaster a huge closed mouth grin on her face and speak if spoken to and do her best not to offend anyone while she waited for the effects of the drive to wear off. Sadly, Goldie didn't have this luxury and Florence worried that the old woman's dentures would fly out of her mouth the minute her tight lips released their grip.

"Well, look what the cat dragged in!" Della said as she opened the screen door to let Goldie and Florence pass through without a preamble. "Miss Goldie, you decide to go work for Mr. Hardy?" Della teased as the women found a place to sit among Della's sisters.

Card tables pushed end to end ran the length of the living room stacked high with rippling green stamp books. The smell of wet paper, glue and cigarette smoke blended with fresh cut grass on the breezes blowing through the open windows throughout the house.

"Y'all find some place to sit. June clear off a place for Miss Goldie and Florence. Can I get y'all something to drink? I was just about to fix some more tea. We've just 'bout drank a gallon working on these stamps." Della said as she puttered around the kitchen opening and closing cabinet doors and filling a pot with water to brew tea. Her sisters kept right on working licking stamps and placing them in the stamp-sized grids on the pages of the books.

"What are y'all saving for? Must've got something in mind to be working so hard." Goldie said as she thumbed through the S & H Stamp Ideabook. Florence picked up the catalogue closest to her and began doing the same. Florence never had the patience to save stamps but admired those that did. She did, however, enjoy dreaming her way through the glossy pages of the catalogue. Buying a week's worth of groceries for a handful of stamps only to put them in a drawer or shoebox and wait until you had enough to fill however many books it would take to buy a deep fryer or lawn chair or alarm clock was just not as satisfying to her as it was to go up on the Square any given Saturday morning and walk into Delray's Furniture Store or Ben Franklin's and pay cash for what she wanted or needed.

"An air conditioner." Della answered from the kitchen.

Her sisters smiled and nodded in agreement. Their sticky smiles and glossy eyes reflecting the lingering effects of the stamp glue that coated their tongues.

"Air conditioner you say?" Goldie asked.

"Yeah, Kitty got one last year. We saved the whole year for her to get one. Not sure how it was that she went first..." Della stopped to recall why her younger sister was the first to get the window unit air conditioner.

"It was my idea and I had more books than y'all." Kitty said with a slight slur. The glue making her tongue too lazy to form words.

None of the sisters disagreed too busy licking and sticking and hoping to be next year's recipient of the air conditioner.

"That's right. She had been working on that idea for some time. I had said something to Sturgill about us getting one of those window units, just a small one, like they've got on the wall in Delray's and he'd have nothing of it. Said that'll be the death of people sitting in artificial cool air. Well, you know Sturg. Can't argue with him once he has laid down the law." Della said as she filled glasses with ice and tea.

"But if he doesn't like the idea, how come you are going to put all your stamps toward an air conditioner?" Florence asked testing her jaw to make sure she wasn't going to bite her tongue.

The sisters eyeballed one another knowing the answer but being caught up in the momentum of getting all the stamp books filled neither stopped leaving Della to continue the conversation.

"Sturgill's problem was spending the money and going into Delray's to buy it. He just ain't got the stomach for doing things he thinks would make him look uppity to folks." Della paused to take a long drink of tea. The lemon wedge floating near the rim making her look like she had a yellow mustache. "He's not going to give two hoots about having a window unit as long as it ain't him that's got to be bothered with the getting part. And, between me and my sisters here, I'll have enough to get one this year and they'll be here to help get it in the window."

Goldie kept thumbing through the Ideabook and sipping on ice tea. "Virginia and Kathleen done been here and gone?" She asked not taking her eyes off the page. She knew it would start a stir and it was best to not make eye contact with any one of the sisters.

The sisters sat slack-jawed waiting for Della to respond. Laughing to herself to keep from airing the family's dirty laundry, Della said, "No we ain't interesting enough for those two." She laughed again at a private thought. "You know how the young ones are. Thinking what they've got going on is so much more important than anyone else."

Goldie knew she struck a nerve but she also knew she

hadn't goaded Della enough. Pushing on, still not looking up from the page, "June doesn't seem to have any trouble helping out." She said drawing attention to Della's niece. June flushed pink at the mention of her name. She had been working quietly helping out. Trying to stay busy hoping that one day her aunts would remember her allegiance and return the favor. Maybe, June hoped privately, she would one day be on the receiving end of the family's collection of S & H Green Stamps.

"June is a good one." Della said proudly. Goldie agreed. They all agreed. "Can't say the same for those other two. They're thick as thieves."

Goldie smiled returning the S & H Green Stamp Idea-book to the coffee table. Florence had been watching and listening to the exchange. She almost spewed ice tea out of her mouth when she heard Della say thieves. That was the opening Goldie was waiting for and just like any beast of prey, she pounced on it.

"Well, speaking of thieves," Goldie stretched her legs out in front of her, then pulled them back into a cross-legged position imitating Della. "I don't 'reckon you'd know anything about that new man Roy Chilton has got working over at his place, do you? Saw him this morning for the first time. Curious looking fellar."

Della thought for a second. "You wouldn't be speaking of that man that's come up from Nashville would you? I 'reckon he's been working over there near on a month maybe two."

Goldie waited without answering giving Della the advantage of the conversation.

"I guess it's been a week maybe longer. I ran into Dorothy over at the A&P. We were talking a spell and she came around to telling me about this here fellar from Nashville walked up to the place there one evening just 'fore they were about to close down for the night asking Roy if he knew of anyone looking for an extra set of hands. Well, Roy being the kind not to turn a man away, sat for a spell jawing with the fellar. Dorothy said she went on up to the house figuring they were going to be a while. She said when Roy came in later on he told her he hired the man to help out at the station and to do some work on the farm."

Della stopped to refill her glass of tea and to offer everyone else a refill. Goldie sat with the look of ease and obvious expectation that once Della replenished her sisters' drinks so they could be on about their stamp licking, she would commence to finishing her story. Florence was spellbound by the whole proceeding and sat quietly in amazement.

"I let Dorothy finish her story figuring she had been holding on to the information for so long she needed to unload it on someone before I commenced to asking her questions. I figured she knew more than what she had said and just needed a little help in finding her way. She was right nervous about it all, I'd say." Della took a long sip of tea. The lemon mustache resting across her upper lip.

"Nervous you say?" Goldie asked keeping Della on point.

"Yeah, nervous, like she was not too sure about this fellar. So I asked her about him. What she knew about him. With all that carrying on down in Nashville. Well, you just can't be too safe is what I say." Della announced and her sisters hummed in agreement. "You ain't going to believe what she told me. She said this man had been to the hospital down there in Nashville. That he had been a patient there and was told they had done all they could do for him. I don't recollect what the doctors told him he had. Can't say I recollect Dorothy saying. But, she said he told Roy that he had enough of the place and just got up and walked out." Della paused as everyone in the room gasped with surprise. "I don't know how he ended up here but that's the long and short of it."

Goldie waited for Della to retrieve any further information from her memory to let the idea of a stranger in the community settle on everyone's mind. "Did she happen to say when all this took place? Couldn't be recently could it. Surely he's been around longer than a month. Did you say he'd been working at the station a month?" Goldie was fitting together her timeline.

Della studied on it a while and then said, "You know

now that you mention it. I believe Dorothy said she figured he'd only be staying around a month or two." Della thought some more. "That's right. Seems like Roy gave her the impression this fellar wasn't going to be around long. Like he was just passing through, as they say. But that was back at the first of the year. And, he's still here."

Goldie got up. Stretched her back out. Looking to Florence, she announced it was time they were heading back to town before Ben got to thinking they've ran off with his truck and business. Everyone laughed at the thought knowing Ben Hardy had been sweet on Goldie for years and would give her the shirt off his back, not that she needed another man's shirt, if she showed him the slightest interest in him or his shirt.

Walking Florence and Goldie to the edge of the front porch, Della thanked them for stopping by for the visit, "Y'all come back when you can stay longer. Florence, tell Ruskin we said hey."

Florence said she would.

"Tell Sturgill we'll talk to him the next." Goldie shouted over the truck engine.

Della waved and watched as the truck bounced out of sight. She was in the house and counting finished stamp books before it dawned on her that Goldie never said why she and Florence came by and what she meant about calling that Nashville man a thief.

Chapter Thirteen

"Son, looks like something has eat your legs alive." Arvis croaked like a toad. Pulling his long overall straps over his short shoulders and fastening them. His squinty eyes still full of sleep and his cold vocal chords made him look and sound like a toad. A toad in overalls. Sunrise had not reached the depths of the hollow but the day's work never waited on the sun.

Sonny sat on the truck tailgate. His pants legs pushed to his knees inspecting his bare legs for scabbed over bug bites. "Fleas."

"Go to bed with dogs." Arvis said wiping the grin from his face with his dirty hand. Sonny could never tell if the man was laughing at him or with him. "I said when you should up here six, seven months ago if you want to sleep in the house you can."

"I 'preciate it but the Ford works just fine." Sonny said picking at a scab on his forearm.

"Suit y'self. Got coffee in the pot and biscuits on the table. I'll be back directly."

Sonny's stomach growled on cue. Watching the old man's truck stir up a dust cloud past the milk barn and tobacco barn, he waited until the truck's taillights were well out of sight before he made his way to the house. Stomping his feet to scare away the rats, Sonny grabbed the first cup he saw, poured coffee, filled his pockets with cold biscuits and left the house as quickly as he entered. He didn't know much about the nature of rats but he knew anything getting a free meal isn't going to run too far from the table.

Back on the truck's tailgate, the sun sliding over the rusted barn peaks, the bird dogs running back down the road from chasing after Arvis's truck, Sonny knew he had just enough time to eat the cold biscuits before the dogs came sniffing around for their share. Playing last night's conversation over in his head like a broken record, Sonny chewed on cold biscuits and Arvis's cold comfort. Arvis had gone too far joking about the possibility of Jimbo Bishop picking up where he left off before Sonny and Kathleen got married. He tried to convince Sonny that Jimbo had taken up with Kathleen again. The old man's words worried him, *"You ain't dead a year and already the hounds are circling."* Sonny could still see Arvis picking at his rotting teeth with the same end of his pocket knife he had just cleaned axil grease from under his fingernails as if the words had been lodged there like a piece of gristle. He spat and drove his point home in the event Sonny didn't get it the first time around. *"It's a pity. Skin that soft begs to be touched. I reckon it's just nature."* Sonny regretted his reaction. Regretted it last night and again this morning as he remembered it all. He knew from experience the best way to handle this brand of humor was to not let it get to you. He knew if he couldn't laugh along the next best thing he should have done was to sit stone silent but instead he flinched. Flinched like a schoolgirl getting her braids pulled by the playground bully. *"You understand nature don't you boy? A woman ain't going to wait around. 'Specially one that's done been married. Like your Kathleen. Ain't got nothing to do with proper. Proper is what the preacher wants you to study on. But, I tell you truth. As true as the nose on your face, if you plan to keep that woman much longer you best be figuring out what you're doin' here."*

The dogs sat patiently at Sonny's dangling feet watching and waiting for Sonny to drop a crumb. Beggars the lot of them. He had spent the night tossing and turning and fighting for space in the truck bed with the flea infested hounds and here they were this morning inching in expectantly. Sonny lost sleep thinking about what the old man had said. If he didn't put the thoughts out of his mind. If he didn't shut out everything Arvis had said. Everything he implied. Sonny knew he would be ate up with regret like he was ate up with fleas. He needed to get busy. Busy forgetting.

Arvis drove around town looking for cast offs. Large household items left by the road in neighborhoods by families that had gotten in the habit of buying new instead of repairing what they had. It was trash day. If he got there before the trash man, he could get his hands on things that in his opinion needed a little attention and would be good as new. His yard was littered with these sorts of great finds. Sprawled out like a blanket between Shepherd's Gap and Hood's Bluff, the grass on Arvis Ange's property had long since died from lack of sunlight under junk cars, piles of scrap metal, leftover lumber, broken furniture and worn out appliances.

Spying a wringer washing machine at the end of a driveway, Arvis pulled his truck over and began giving the washer the once over. One look to the machine. Two looks to the house.

"Arvis? You doin' alright this morning'" Morgan Bishop said making his way down his drive way. Although he wasn't scheduled to be at the funeral home until later that afternoon, he had already dressed in his regulation black suit and tie.

"Fair to middlin'. Fair to middlin'." Arvis answered trying not to appear frustrated that he wasn't able to retrieve the cast off appliance without making polite conversation.

"Had to replace her. Think you can get a part or two off her, you're welcome to her." Morgan said lighting a cigarette and stroking the broken wringer arm on the washing machine as if it was aware of his intentions.

"I 'spect she's got a few good parts left in her. Why don't you give me a hand and I'll be on my way." Arvis grumbled.

With one lift and two steps the two men loaded the washing machine in the bed of the truck. Arvis touched the brim of his hat stained with grease and sweat and turned toward the truck cab but stopped short of climbing inside.

"Bishop?" Arvis turned back suddenly recognizing the washer's owner.

"Yep." Morgan stopped, dropped the butt of the cigarette on the street and snuffed it out with the toe of his wingtip.

"I thought that was you. Haven't seen you in a month of Sundays. How you doing? I didn't know you lived in town. Why did I think you lived over the funeral parlor?" Arvis said as if struck with sudden curiosity and hospitality.

"Yep. We did back when the boys were little. With young'un's running around we had to find a place that wasn't so disruptive to doing business. We've been here going on ten maybe twelve years." Morgan said.

"That long you say?" Arvis asked. His mind knitting a scheme as he made his way back to his truck cab. "Your boy still working for the law?"

Bishop nodded accustom to innocuous small talk and assuming the conversation was ending as he stood in the street waiting for Arvis to pull away. Arvis eyed him. His scheme building steam with thoughts of the Bishop boy and Kathleen Price.

"Reckon that keeps him busy?"

"Pretty busy." Morgan said lighting another cigarette. Years spent in the funeral business had left him with a nervous disposition and a chain-smoking habit.

"Reckon the sheriff has got them all busy running the roads looking for the Price boy?" Arvis casted his line waiting for Morgan to bite.

"Best I know, they called off that search some time ago." Morgan stopped, rubbed the razor burn on his jaw and chin, pulled a long drag off his cigarette, exhaled and said. "I believe Kathleen told the sheriff there was no point in looking. If I'm not mistaken," he rested the cigarette in the corner of his mouth, his long eyelashes folding against the rising smoke, he looked at his watch but didn't read the time another of his ticks, "she didn't think it was in the best interest of the sheriff's time. But, just between you and me and the fence post," he exhaled taking the cigarette from his mouth, "I don't think the sheriff paid her no mind 'cause he's got Jimbo circling by there at least once if not twice a week."

"By where?" Arvis asked as if he didn't follow.

"By Kathleen Price's place, got him checking on things there, you know, just in case Sonny-boy finds his way back home. You know what they say about the apple falling." Morgan said snuffing out the cigarette.

"Now wait a minute. Are you telling me Ruskin has got

your boy going out to the Flats twice a week to see about Kathleen Price on the chance that Sonny might show back up? I heard tale that car burned out so badly nothing or no one could have walked away from it and survived, sure as not these past several months." Arvis said almost convincing himself.

"You know as well as I do Sonny-boy Price lands on his feet. Like I said, he is just like his daddy. Tinkum could get in all kinds of trouble and be well in over his head and find his way out as if nothing ever happened and look better for it." Morgan said lighting another cigarette.

Arvis didn't appreciate Morgan casting aspersions on the dead or at least the presumed dead. Arvis knew Sonny wasn't dead and he knew Tinkum wasn't dead. Was Morgan trying to tell him, he also knew the two were not dead? Did his business dealings run deeper than laying out the dead and burying them?

Trusting his sense of humor to get him out of sticky situations, Arvis joked, "Yeah, old Tinkum sure could find his way into a mess. And, you're right about him coming out on the tail end looking better than when he went in, that's for sure."

The two men laughed. Each enjoying private thoughts and recollections.

"Well, I wouldn't be surprised if we don't see them both sometime on down the road." Morgan said repeating his ritual with the cigarette and watch.

Arvis had enough. He was never fond of Morgan Bishop. He didn't care for him when they were coming up as boys and he hadn't learned to like him over time. For Arvis, Morgan Bishop was like most people in Tillman, he was a means to an end. A necessary relationship for services rendered.

Arvis smiled, touched his hat again and drove off leaving Bishop staring at the truck and his old washing machine with its broken wringer arm bouncing like it was waving goodbye.

* * *

Rolling down the hill to the holler where his place rested in the shadow of two of the Scots Ridge's highest hills, Arvis

Ange's mouth watered with news he couldn't wait to impart to his resident squatter.

"You been staying busy?" Arvis asked bringing the truck to stop between two walnut trees in what would be his front yard if it wasn't for the jungle of junk.

"Been stacking that pile of two by fours. How about you? Looks like a good load there." Sonny said marveling at the mound of household goods swelling over the truck bed and tailgate.

"It'll keep. You ate? I stopped in at Sweetie's. Had a taste for bar-b-que.   Turn that bucket over there and pull it up here and let's eat." Arvis said pulling a grease stained paper bag from the truck seat.

Sonny squatted under the walnut tree and helped himself to bar-b-que sandwiched between cornbread patties wrapped in wax paper. Thankful for the wax paper when he saw that Arvis had not washed his hands. Arvis waddled back over to the truck and pulled out two RC Colas using the open truck door to pop off the caps leaving them where they landed.

"Sweetie knows her way around a hog. That's for sure." Arvis said. Bar-b-que sauce running down his chin from the corner of his mouth.

"And the kitchen too, this cornbread is nothing to sneeze at." Sonny volleyed paying closer attention to his meal and not his present company in an effort to enjoy the food and not lose his appetite.

"Saw Morgan Bishop in town." Arvis said with a belch.

"We going to beat that dead horse again?" Sonny said full of food and confidence.

"Just making conversation. That's all."

Arvis let some time pass and let Sonny finish his lunch while the idea wormed its way in wiggling around festering up ideas that only Sonny could create. Arvis was planting the seed. Sonny was cultivating it.

Breaking the silence and tension, Sonny played right into Arvis's hand, "Why would I care about anything Morgan Bishop had to say?"

Arvis laughed between the two last swigs of his RC. "I figure you being a dead man and all. You'd have an interest in the funeral parlor business and the man that runs it." Arvis choked on his laughter.

Sonny cleared his throat, spit and stomped off to finish sorting the mix matched lumber. Biding his time and letting his food digest, Arvis eased off the overturned bucket, stretched out in the shade of the tree and took a nap, leaving Sonny to his thoughts and his penance.

* * *

The day had waned and so had the work. Sonny had exhausted not only his body but also his mind. He had broken a promise to himself. Something he was getting too good at doing. He had let Arvis Ange get under his skin one too many times. He knew when he decided to take refuge at the old man's junkyard earlier in the year that if he was to survive he would have to lower his standards. Standards that by anyone else's measure where already below respectable. He knew the old man was well versed in misery and could spot the likeness in others. It was a mystery of human nature. A mystery Sonny had learned too early in life. Without the benefit of a protective father and loving mother to guide him through life's obstacles, he became a man on the handouts of others. Being tossed from pillar to post, living first with one then another, he quickly learned he could only trust himself and to appreciate the kindness of others while knowing when one hand may be feeding you the other is expecting recompense. Life had taught him no matter what anyone said while they offered you a place to lay your head or food to fill your belly or the shirt off their back, if you didn't pay close attention to what the other hand, the supposedly idle hand empty of grace its counterpart so freely offered, you would soon find it tossing you out, asking for payment, or stripping you naked of self-respect. It was that hand Sonny knew best. It was by that hand he had suffered the most.

Arvis knew Sonny's history. He knew Sonny's people. He knew the circumstances behind the rumors and Arvis knew, like a handful of others that had made promises to raise the boy to a man, just how far to push him, to steer him, to guide Sonny in the way he should go. It was an investment that had so far paid little dividends but Arvis and the others were not ready to give up.

"Got the stuff off the truck." Sonny said as he made his way back to the shade of the trees where Arvis had been napping.

"You waiting on a re-ward?" Arvis said scratching his head from sleeping on the ground.

"Just being helpful. That's all." Sonny mumbled.

"Helpful's good. Helpful's good." Arvis encouraged feeling the tension radiating.

"Think you might be going into town again tomorrow?" Sonny said leaning against the truck.

Arvis raised up on his heels. Wobbled a bit and flopped back to a reclined position. Sonny wanted to laugh but didn't dare. He could see the old man landed harder than he expected possibly bruising his hip and definitely bruising his pride. "Maybe. You got business in town?"

"Maybe." Sonny said still nursing his hurt feelings.

"You've got my attention. Best to get on with it." Arvis said, rubbing his rump from the short tumble.

"I was just thinking you might want to do some trading."

"I'm listening." Arvis said rolling onto his back and closing his eyes. Sonny wasn't sure he should continue on with his plan. He wrestled with whether to go over and help the man to his feet and get him inside or to leave well enough alone. He couldn't risk shaming the old man or making him angry.

"I was just thinking I can't do enough work around here to repay you for all you've done for me. Letting me stay without question and not saying anything to anyone in town about me being here. I appreciate your help and your respect and just felt I could do more than I'm doing for you."

Arvis chuckled. "Son, let me stop you right there before you shine your tongue past the point of speaking the truth. There's plenty work around here for a hundred men so don't go on about there not being enough for repayment. I don't recollect charging you to stay here but I do respect a man's need to earn his keep." Arvis said, his arm resting over his eyes. "Now, if you want to discuss a trade. I'm all ears. Let's hear it."

"I was just thinking on what I left behind."

"Now you're talking. Go ahead."

"I left a barn full of tools. A couple of guns. A car. It's up on blocks but."

"Uh, uh. Go ahead." Arvis's face broke into a smile.

"I was just thinking. If you were out and about and found yourself over in Mud Flats over by my place, you could stop in and make a trade with Kathleen."

"Uh, uh. I'm listening." Arvis said. His mind two steps ahead.

"I'll work off my room and board here and you can trade her things she may need for what I left behind."

Arvis rolled over onto his side. His bulk robbing his lungs of sufficient space making him wheeze. "Sort of like you was still taking care of it. Is that what you're getting at? I convince her to trade your goods for things you just happen to send by me. Is that it?"

Sonny nodded. It sounded different coming from Arvis. In Sonny's head, it sounded wholesome and helpful. From Arvis's mouth it sounded conniving and distrustful.

"And what if she's not needing anything? What if she already has someone providing what she needs?" Arvis goaded.

Feeling backhanded Sonny said. "We'll cross that bridge when we get to it. Are you in or not."

"I'm in. Now help me up from here." Arvis grunted.

Chapter Fourteen

Ellis Hatch pushed through the underbrush climbing to the top of Hood's Bluff. He had slowly cut a footpath over the last few months trudging up to the cave where Tinkum Price had been hiding out. Every other trip up the steep hillside, he hoped would be his last. Ellis wasn't one to complain. He never saw any value in it. But, today, he had plenty to complain about when he slipped ripping the knees open in his jeans and ripping the hide off his hand. The hand that had carried the burlap sack he held up above the wet brush to keep the light bread tucked inside from getting soggy.

At the top, Ellis looked around and could see all of Tillman and most of Fulton. He thought to himself that he could never get tired of this view. It was worth the climb on a good day and could turn a bad day around. Standing there taking in the sights with no sounds, people milling about several hundred feet below, like ants running in and out of their little ant holes, Ellis felt like he too could just call it quits and stay up on the bluff, hide out in one of the caves, and let life and the world pass him right on by. For that brief moment, he understood why Tinkum found it easier to run than to face the choices he had made in life. And, he understood better, why Sonny always chose running from responsibility than just sticking it out and seeing things through to the end.

For as long as Ellis could remember, he just took for granted that Tinkum and Sonny were weaker than most men. Their selfish behavior gave no one room to believe otherwise. But, standing up on Hood's Bluff and seeing for himself how separated he was from all of life playing out below him, watching from a distance, never hearing what anyone was saying, whether good or bad, never worrying about whether you did or didn't do the right thing, he could see how that had to take more courage than he had given them credit. He knew when it came down to it, he couldn't do it. For him, he'd rather stand and fight risking everything than to run and hide losing it all.

"What you got there?" Tinkum said stretching. His bare chest so bony Ellis could count every rib. Ellis cringed to see the old man still wearing the stolen coveralls. With them rolled down to his waist, the sleeves tied around him like a belt, Tinkum looked more like a child playing dress up than a grown man in work clothes.

"Brought you some food." Ellis said tossing the sack towards Tinkum then regretting it. He had just spent the better part of the morning treating that sack like it held a litter of newborn kittens then without thought he just tossed it. Letting it lay where it fell.

Tinkum read the changes in Ellis's face. It was a gift. He could read the slightest change in any man's face or the smallest of gestures. It was something he used to his advantage more times than not at the gambling tables, pool halls and back alleys but it was also something he wanted to ignore. There were times when he wished he hadn't seen a twitch of the cheek, a throbbing vein or change in a man's eyes or a woman's heart. But those were things he had learned to live with as best he could. Can't go back and change what was.

"I said you didn't have to keep doing this." Tinkum said squatting to untie the burlap sack heavy with supplies. "You're going to get yourself hurt. Or worse, get yourself mixed up in something you can't get yourself out of." Tinkum slowly and deliberately emptied the sack of its contents one by one. Laying out the loaf of light bread, the chub of bologna and the block of cheese. Turning the sack up on its end, he shook out a pair of jeans, a white oxford shirt, pair of socks and a can of shoe polish.

Looking up at Ellis he said, "Now what in the world am I supposed to do with these?"

"Wear them." Ellis said looking at the old man his body bowed with age and illness. Ellis found it harder and harder to look at Tinkum. It seemed to him each time he hiked the three miles up to the bluff from his place in the Flats, Tinkum had gotten smaller, frailer. In spite of the food he was bringing him on a regular basis and in spite of the work Tinkum was doing at Chilton's service station, he appeared to be getting worse not better.

Tinkum left the clothes laying where they landed and gathered the food up in his hard skinny arms and carried it to the entrance of the cave. The cave he had called home since Thanksgiving. Cutting a slice of bologna and cheese with his pocket knife, he laid out the meat on one slice of bread resting on his left knee and the cheese on the other slice of bread on his right knee, then wiped his knife clean on his britches leg and closed it with the same attention he had used when seducing a woman or petting the head of his sleeping child.

Ellis felt underappreciated in seeing the clothes laying on the wet ground. He had gone to a lot of trouble to buy the clothes at Newberry's, sneak them home and then sneak them out of his home and up to the ill-mannered old man. He didn't have to do any of this and he knew better than to say anything because Tinkum would be quick to point out he never asked for Ellis's help. Sitting there beside the old man, Ellis wondered why he was taking such risks in helping someone who didn't appreciate it and someone who really didn't want or need his help. He wondered why he kept putting himself in these situations over and over again with the Price men.

"How's Virginia?" Tinkum asked. His mouth full of sandwich.

"Busy. She stays busy." Ellis answered without thought.

"And, Kathleen? How is she doing?" Tinkum asked. Biting off another mouthful.

Ellis nodded thoughtlessly, "Busy."

Tinkum washed the last of his bologna and cheese sandwich down with what remained in the bottle of Johnnie Walker red he had shoved into his boot. With the bottle empty, he tossed it to the side sending it crashing into the cave wall and shattering. Ellis took this all in but was not really seeing it lost in thought.

"Cat got your tongue boy? You look like you're studying awfully hard on something. You got something to say?" Tinkum said pushing himself up to a somewhat standing position. His body showing the effects of living on the run. Pale pocked scars littered his torso drawing attention away from the hearts tattooed on his forearms. Each with a woman's name scrolled across its middle. Shuffling to the back of the cave, he dug around his belongings until he found another bottle of whiskey. Breaking the seal, he took a deep drink, screwed the cap back on and pushed the bottle into his boot where the other had been and returned to where he had been sitting.

Pushing tobacco deep into the chamber of his pipe, Tinkum struck a match and sucked on the pipe bit pulling the flame into the tobacco. The warm sweet smell of cherries wrapped around them.

"Don't that bother your breathing?" Ellis asked remembering Tinkum's story months ago about walking out of the hospital in Nashville. His lungs too damaged by disease the doctors couldn't do anything for him.

"Nah, the heat feels good. Helps me breathe." Tinkum said drawing in a mouthful of sweet cherry flavored smoke. "It's like the cave. The damp helps me keep my breath."

"How is it again you said you came to be in that hospital?" Ellis asked. He had heard the story more times than he could count but he needed to hear it one more time. He was listening for hole in the story. Some little detail to tell him that as usual Tinkum was blowing more than tobacco smoke.

"Work detail. Got sick on the work detail." Tinkum said.

"Work detail." Ellis repeated. "From the prison, you said?" He just had to ask again. He didn't believe the old man had been in the state penitentiary. Something about his story just didn't add up.

"Yep, that's right." Tinkum said. "They had us working in the field when I took to coughing. Well, I reckon it scared the old straw boss because before I knew what was what they had me in a truck and on the way to the hospital." Tinkum enjoyed his pipe waiting for Ellis to ask his next question. He felt it coming. He could read it on the boy's face.

"And you said, that's where you ran into your cousin, at the hospital? He was the one that told you about Kathleen expecting?" Ellis asked finishing the story.

"Yep, that's right too. It was my cousin. They put me in

one of those wards but only two beds was occupied at the time, his and mine. We commenced to visiting and one thing led to another and before we knew it, we were exchanging names and places, and that's when we made the connection. A family as big as ours, can't say you see or know all your people at first glance but give a man a minute or two and you'll soon find out you're related." Tinkum explained.

"And, that's how you found out about Kathleen and the baby?" Ellis asked again.

"Nah, now that's not a hundred percent correct. That's where I found out that they was expecting, Sonny and Kathleen, that is. My cousin said that he had just been moved from the hospital here to the one down there in Nashville for some tests they didn't have the right doctor or equipment for here. He was asking if I was going to be out of the hospital in time to see the baby. Me not knowing what baby he was talking about, I said I didn't rightly know. He said he sure hoped I was home in time. That it would be a crying shame to miss seeing my first grandchild." Tinkum said. Crossing his arms over his crossed legs. He looked like a twisted bag of bones.

"And, so that's when you decided to head back this way?" Ellis asked knowing the answer.

"Yep, that's right. Them there doctors had done all they could do. I had no intentions of spending my last days in the pen and if I got caught, well I would just get caught, but I was determined to see my first grandchild. So, once everything got still and everyone was good and asleep, I traded my hospital gown for my cousin's clothes hanging on the hook by his bed and walked out of the hospital just like I walked in." Tinkum said then corrected himself. "I take that back. I wasn't wearing chains when I walked out."

Ellis still didn't believe the man had been in prison. If there was any truth in it or not he wasn't sure but as long as he didn't have proof, he felt better thinking that part of the story was just made up to once again add a little spice and interest to Tinkum's otherwise sad and miserable life. When he ran out on his family and friends twenty some odd years ago, he left little room or opportunity to come back without making the life he ran to sound bigger than the one he left behind. Too many broken hearts and balled-up fists were waiting on him otherwise.

"So, have you been by the house to see Melody?" Ellis asked another obvious question.

"Nah, can't say I have." Tinkum said studying the sky as if looking for answers.

"You get any further than Chilton's or the judge's?" Ellis said pushing his luck.

"Make it down to Chilton's every day. He's got me running errands and patching tires. Can't say I've been by Henry's." Tinkum said. The corner of his mouth curling into a soft smile. He knew what the boy was trying to do. He had been pressing him for months about not wearing Judge Filbry's coveralls saying the cousin's clothes should be enough or to wear some of the store bought clothes. Fearing Goldalena would recognize the coveralls and want to know who was wearing them and how he came to have them on, Ellis was determined to give Tinkum every chance to say he took them from the Filbry's and every chance to wear something else even if it meant he bought every pair of jeans at Newberry's.

"Can't say or won't say?" Ellis asked.

"Not sure there's a difference." Tinkum answered.

"You know as soon as she sees you in the judge's coveralls she is going to call the law. It's not like Ruskin isn't already two steps ahead of everyone when it comes to finding Sonny. Now with you in town and wearing Judge Filbry's coveralls right out in public for the whole world to see. You might as well be asking for it." Ellis said building up a head of steam.

Laughing to himself and at the boy, Tinkum asked, "Asking for what, you reckon?"

"Asking to go back to the pen for starters!" Ellis said frustrated.

Feeling sure of himself and enjoying the tangle of conversation Tinkum turned the tables on Ellis. "What makes you think Goldie is going to recognize these here coveralls? I don't recollect seeing her and if I did, how is she going to know these are Henry's?"

"So are you admitting that they are?" Ellis said almost swallowing his tongue in surprise.

"Nah, you're saying they are. I'm asking you how would she know they are his." Tinkum asked.

"Because she said they are!" Ellis shouted. Dropping his head into his hands, he took several deep breaths before attempting to lift his head and explain. When he did Tinkum was sitting there beside of him waiting as though nothing out of the ordinary had just happened. "She said she saw you. She has been talking to everyone that will listen that back in the winter someone stole a pair of coveralls from her cellar. Just a week or so ago, she added to her story that she saw the coveralls on a man Chilton had working for him. She was there at Chilton's and saw you in the coveralls. It won't take her long before she puts two and two together and figures out it was you." Ellis said. His voice catching in his throat with emotion.

"You said she saw me?" Tinkum asked. His taunt face bright with ideas.

Ellis managed a nod too exhausted to repeat himself.

Scratching his balding head with the ring finger on his left hand, he thought for a second or two, giving Ellis time to settle down and time for his thoughts to come together. Emptying the pipe in the palm of his hand and tossing out the last remaining ashes, he pulled out his pocketknife and scraped the chamber clean.

Ellis waited for Tinkum to speak. He had nothing more to say. It was up to the old man to say what happens next. There was nothing more Ellis could do. He could keep bringing food up the hill, he could keep risking buying new clothes that would never replace the coveralls, he could keep making up stories of where he had been and why, but sooner or later, it was up to Tinkum to decide if he was staying or going. It was up to Tinkum whether he got caught pushing the limits of everyone's hospitality.

Sonny was out there somewhere. Ellis was sure of it. They had practiced the roll out for years. They'd done it for fun. They'd done it for the risk. Sonny had done it to save his life.

Here Ellis sat, with Sonny's dad trying to save his life. It was more than one man could handle.

Chapter Fifteen

Florence hung up the phone receiver just as the music ended and the soft baritone voice she waited to hear all day announced The Secret Storm. Ruskin called to say he wouldn't be home for supper. She had forgotten why that used to upset her. Now she takes it in stride. The food will keep. Her Tupperware would make sure the meatloaf tasted as good warmed over as when it came out of the oven. Same for her baked beans and the cheesy potatoes she was trying out from the recipe she found in this month's Woman's Day.

The ironing board was set up in front of the television. The brown paper grocery sacks filled with damp clothes she had sprinkled were waiting in the refrigerator. She plugged the iron in and waited for it to get hot. Lost in the world of Woodbridge, she imagined Peter Ames dropping by for supper and if he would like her cheesy potatoes.

Standing in the center of the living room, in front of the picture window Florence noticed Goldie packing boxes in the backseat of her Buick. Curiosity was getting the best of her but she couldn't miss a minute of the treasured time she spent keeping up with the Ames family. Once the ironing was finished and everything was hanging in the closet, she would go over and see what Goldie was up to but not a minute sooner. She paced her ironing to the length of the soap opera and only stepped away from the ironing board or television during commercials. Goldie, like everything else would have to wait.

* * *

"So you got it worked out for me?" Goldie wiped the sweat from her brow as she caught her breath. Sitting on the kitchen stool under the telephone, she sipped on ice water.

"She'll be ready. I think it will do her some good. Give her something to do to keep things off her mind. Nothing worse than fretting over something you can't change. If that boy is serious about marrying her, she'll soon find out, but she don't need to sit around worrying about it." Della said. She too was sitting in her kitchen waiting for her husband to come in from the fields for his supper. The late afternoon breezes moved her kitchen curtains like sails on a ship. In and out the red-checkered cotton fabric lifted off the window screen and then pressed against it. The curtains distracted her from the telephone conversation and made her wonder when she last took down the curtains and washed them. One thought led to another and before she knew it she was no longer listening to Goldalena but was making plans to take down all the curtains in the house to wash them and the windows and the screens.

"Well, I won't keep you. I'll be by there sometime tomorrow. I've got to get the rest of my strawberries up and then I'll be by there to pick her up. You tell June I sure appreciate the help. It'll be good for us both. I've got enough work around here to keep her and ten more just like her busy well past summer." Goldie laughed chewing ice.

"See you then." Della said hanging up the phone and making a beeline to the kitchen curtains.

Across the street, Florence was putting away the ironing board setting the iron on the deep freeze in the garage to cool. She had burned herself one too many times leaving the iron on the kitchen counter and forgetting that it could still be hot. Now, she puts it out in the garage on the deep freeze where she won't risk getting burned while it cools.

"Florence!" Goldie called from the living room. The old woman had been in and out of the Bright's home for years and had made herself welcome to walk in without being let in by Florence or Ruskin.

"Out here!" Florence shouted. Noticing the garage could use a good sweeping, Florence was in the throes of piling a mountain of dust when Goldie came out of the kitchen door holding two jars of strawberry jam.

"Brought you and Ruskin some jam. Decided to make jam this year instead of preserves. Let me know what you think." Goldie stood on the step holding the screen door open with her elbow a jar of jam in each hand.

"Oh, you didn't have to do that Goldie. I think we are still eating on the last bit you gave us last year." Florence said making the customary thank you.

"No need being stingy with it. I've got plenty and you're welcome to it." Goldie said. Watching and waiting for her neighbor to finish her chore and sit a while and gossip.

Florence stopped sweeping long enough to take the two jars of jam from Goldie. "Sit a spell. I'm going to finish up this floor and then we'll go in and have some supper. Have you ate?"

"Too hot to eat just yet." Goldie said wiping sweat from her brow with her husband's shirtsleeve. She had set aside three shirts that needed buttons or stitch or two on the hem to use as work shirts. The blue striped oxford was her favorite. The color always reminded her of Henry's eyes. The chinos had washed and worn to a rose petal softness. Hitched high upon her waist, covering her round belly and sitting just under her full bust, the pants were a compliment to the shirt both with their ends rolled up for comfort and practicality, the shirt sleeves to the elbow and the pants legs to the ankle.

"Yeah, you've got a point there." Florence said digging her broom into the corners of the garage chipping stubborn dust into the pile. "Almost time to start having a cold plate instead of stoking up the house with a warm supper."

"Gets warmer earlier every year." Goldie said pointing to places Florence had missed.

Stopping long enough to catch her breath and letting the dust settle, Florence asked, "I've been meaning to ask you about our trip up to Della's. After we came back through town, stopped at the A&P and the dry cleaners to pick up the judge's seersucker suit, and then over to Mr. Hardy's to get your Buick, I completely forgot to ask you what it is that you gathered going up there to see Della and her sisters."

"Just got off the phone with Della, now that you mention it. I called her to see what she thought about June coming to stay with me for a while. Help me around the house and such. You'd a thought I had read her mind. She was two steps ahead of me. Before I could get the words out, she was finishing my sentences and moving things right along." Goldie laughed as if remembering a private thought. "She is going to have June packed and ready for me tomorrow sometime. Figure I'll go by there, pick her up and treat her to a milk shake over at Patti Cake's."

Florence started back in to sweeping realizing it was going to take the old woman time to work up to answering her question.

"Having June at the house will be good. You know, she is having a hard time of it right now with Jimbo." Goldie was careful testing the waters with mentioning one of Ruskin's deputies to Florence. Seeing that Florence didn't react to hearing the young deputy's name, she continued. "Yeah, seems the way things are going with him spending so much time upon the ridge, June has taken it into her head that she should call off the wedding."

Resting her forearms on the top of the broom, Florence stopped sweeping and gave her undivided attention to what Goldie was saying.

"Della seems to think getting June out of the house and busy doing something other than sitting around waiting for the phone to ring will help her think through her decision. I don't know how much help I can be about those matters but I can give her a place to stay and plenty to do. She could have stayed at Della's or any of the sisters' but Della seemed to think it would be better if it wasn't someone in the family. Far be it from me to stop progress and like I said, having June at the house will be helpful."

Stepping off the porch, holding the dustpan for Florence to sweep the pile of dirt into it, Goldie made her way around to answering Florence's question. "I reckon it was more about what wasn't said while we were at Della's than it was what was said. Those Hatch girls are quick to pass judgment on anyone and anything contrary to the way they do things. It's just the way they are turned. I blame it on their mama but Ephraim is just as guilty about it. I know for a fact that he is still smarting over the way Tinkum left and that's why he has moved heaven and earth to keep Sonny-boy and Kathleen in that house. It's not any coincidence that Ellis and Virginia are so involved with what goes on with those two. Ephraim has drilled it into those children's heads, especially Ellis, since the day they were old enough to understand that Sonny-boy was one of them, no questions asked. His name might as well be Hatch as far as the Hatch family is concerned. So, it was no mistake that nothing was said when Virginia and Kathleen got brought up but I don't know if you could tell, they had plenty to say." Goldie handed the dustpan to Florence and returned to her place on the porch. Florence emptied the dustpan in the high weeds that ran alongside the empty lot beside the house. Coming back to the garage she pulled up a lawn chair and waited for Goldie to resume.

Laughing Goldie said, "That dust is going to be back in here before you know it."

Florence laughed too and sat quietly letting the old woman find her way back to where she left off.

"I should have known better than to expect them to say anything about Tinkum. I knew it was him in the coveralls. Of course it was him, they are his coveralls." Goldie said as if Florence had questioned her.

Florence sat flabbergasted at what she was hearing. Tinkum Price had left Fulton almost twenty years ago. She knew the rumors and wondered how much truth was in them. Ruskin had said there was trouble between Tinkum Price, Ephraim Hatch, Arvis Ange and Judge Filbry but he never spent enough time on the subject to give Florence any idea what kind of trouble. If Tinkum was back in Fulton, there had to be a reason for it.

"The day Tinkum left town he came by the house to see Henry. At least that is what he said he was doing. When I told this to Henry hours later, he said Tinkum knew Henry wasn't at home because he had just seen him. They had been playing cards to pass the time while a storm passed. By the time Tinkum got down the ridge and over to the house, the storm had passed and Henry and the others were back in the field working. Everyone was back working except Tinkum. He was too busy finding a way out of a day's work. Always was like that, doubt he has changed. He knocked on the door but I was around back working in the cellar. He came as far as the cellar door and asked if I'd mind if he left some things for Henry. Said, he'd be back to get them but just needed a place for them for a while. I was busy making room on the shelves for my canning jars and told him to just leave whatever it was there and I'd make sure Henry got it when he got home. Well, I reckon he was in such a hurry to get going that it didn't dawn on him to be his usually contrary self, because he left the bag where he stood and the next time I looked up he was gone."

Florence's mouth had gone dry from being gaped open. She worked her tongue around trying to soothe her mouth and spit out her question. "What was in the bag?" She asked like a child listening to a ghost story.

"Clothes mostly. The coveralls were part of them. I hung up what I could on hooks and nails in the cellar. Every year Henry would take them out to air and then return them to their hanging place as if in the hopes that one day Tinkum would find his way back and need them." Goldie laughed again at a private thought. "I guess Henry was right."

"Right? Right about what? That Tinkum would come back for his clothes?" Florence asked sitting on the edge of her chair. Her neck stretched forward coaxing the story from Goldie.

"Yep. I reckon that's what he did. The night Sonny had his accident on the ridge was the same night, I reckon Tinkum came to get his things. Except, all he got was his coveralls. My guess is something spooked him or he figured he would find his way back to the cellar for the rest of it." Goldie said.

"So, if Tinkum is back and he has been back all this time, why? Why did he come back and why has he stayed?" Florence asked trying to put two and two together. "I mean, he must know by now that Sonny is gone." Shaking her head mournfully, "It's just sad to think he waited all this time only to come back to loss."

"I can't say why just yet, but I'm telling you now Tinkum coming back and Sonny going missing are tied together somehow. And, that's what I expect June is going to help me find out." Goldie said standing and stretching her tired, stiff muscles.

Chapter Sixteen

The days were getting longer and the mercury was rising proving summer was hot on the trail of spring. The sweet fragrant breezes were now waves of heat and oppressive humidity. Late afternoon showers cropped up to bring some relief only to leave everything in their wake looking like a Turkish steam bath.

Florence would have welcomed the change in temperature when she was June's age but the change of life had brought with it a heat of its own. Not even the air conditioners on display with their billowing streamers at the Western Auto could offer a means of escape.

June loved the weather and took full advantage of it. Days spent swimming at the falls and laying in the sun was just what she needed to get Jimbo off her mind. She appreciated her Aunt Della arranging for her to stay with Mrs. Filbry. She knew there was a lot to learn from spending time with the old woman and plenty of connections in the community to make.

With her bags packed, June sat on her front porch waiting for Goldalena Filbry to pick her up for what she believed to be the chance of a lifetime. Thumbing through the latest edition of Seventeen magazine, daydreaming about life as a Breck girl, June hoped Jimbo would drive by to see her with her suitcase and want to stop and ask what she was up to but before she could play the scenario out in her head of all the things he would say and all the things she would say, Goldalena's Buick rounded the corner.

Smiling and leaning out the car window, Goldie said, "Looks like you're ready to go."

"Yes ma'am." June giggled and put her suitcase in the backseat.

"Well come on. Let's see what we can get ourselves into. I'm thinking a milkshake. How does that sound for a start?" Goldie said waiting for June to settle in to the passenger side of the Buick.

"Sounds good and cold to me." June said trying to be polite and funny at the same time.

It would take some time to find their rhythm but Goldie was looking forward to having the young girl as company. She knew she should feel somewhat guilty for exploiting the situation knowing that a well-placed comment or two would have the girl spilling all she knew or thought she knew about the whereabouts of Tinkum and Sonny Price, but feelings of guilt would have to wait. Wait until she had what she need and then, and only then, would she entertain the idea of guilt.

Nestled in a booth close to the back corner of Patti Cake's Diner, Goldie ordered a chocolate milk shake for herself and left June to order for herself. Patti waited for the girl to make up her mind and made small talk with Goldie.

"No use being shy about it Junebug. Get what you want." Goldie said.

"Nobody calls me that anymore." June said behind the menu sending the two older women into laughter.

"Nothing wrong with a nickname Honey. If it wasn't for a nickname ya'd be sitting at Patti's diner right now. Just don't have the same ring to it does it?" Patti said with a wink.

Goldie laughed enjoying the conversation and company. "No. No. Not the same ring at all."

"You decided Honey?" Patti asked working the last bit of taste out of her Juicy Fruit chewing gum.

"I'll take the cheeseburger plate with a Coke and can I get onion rings with that instead of fries?" June asked placing her order like a truck driver on a long haul.

The two women smiled at her instant confidence and felt good to know they could provide her with a good meal.

Patti scribbled on her order pad, took the menus and said their orders would be right up. Calling out to her husband in the back that an order was on the wheel, she circled the diner filling coffee cups and making conversation with her customers.

"What's this business about Jimbo?" Goldie said, deciding to take the direct approach.

"Jimbo?" June blushed not sure she understood the

question.

"Suit yourself but you've got a captive audience here. I'm as old as dirt and nowhere to be. If you're getting better attention somewhere else let me know and I'll drive ya there." Goldie said teasing the girl into trusting her.

"Ain't getting attention any where's the problem." June said. Her bottom lip pouting as the words dripped from their edge.

"What are you talking about? Pretty girl like you. Getting married and all. You should be meeting yourself coming and going with attention from every direction." Goldie said. Trying to keep the conversation lighthearted. The last thing she needed was to tune the child up into a crying fit right here in the back booth of Patti Cake's.

"You'd think so. And I'd agree. But that's not the case. Least ways not for me." Junes mouth hardly moving to form the words. Her heart beating hard. The pulse throbbing the vein in her neck. Her neck flushed with emotion and embarrassment.

"You telling me that man of yours ain't tripping over himself to spend every minute with you?" Goldie tried to rein in the conversation.

"He did. Not no more."

Patti set the plate of food in front of June and offered Goldie two straws and a long handled spoon for her milkshake. Goldie let June take the time to collect her thoughts and dress her food. After a bite of cheeseburger and washing it down with her Coke, June was ready to open up to her.

"Mama said I should have seen it coming. Said as long as a man is in love he might look at another woman but he can't love another. He told me it was over. Said when Kathleen married Sonny that ended it for him. I believed him. Took him at his word. Everything was well and good. Good for us all. Kathleen and Sonny. Me and Jimbo. But then when the baby got sick, and Sonny. Well, you know Sonny's gone. Anyway. Ever since then Jimbo's been slipping away. Bit by bit slipping from me right back to Kathleen."

Goldie felt badly for the girl and knew it wouldn't take nothing more than something as simple as this to have the Hatch sisters riled up against Kathleen. But what she needed to know, was how Virginia was involved and what the family knew about Sonny's disappearance.

"That is something. I hate to hear it. I'm not going to speak against your mama. A girl needs to trust her mama." Goldie said cajoling the girl. June dipped her onion rings in ketchup and ate them leaving the ice rattling in her empty glass. Patti brought her another Coke and offered Goldie another milkshake but she waved her off.

"That's an awful mess about Sonny. I never did hear when his services were."

"Weren't none." June said between bites of onion rings.

"No service. Folks got to grieve. Got to pay their respects."

"Aunt Della said no body no funeral."

"Your Aunt Della is a good woman. I'm sure she is right." Goldie said trying to piece together the truth while she weeded out the rumors.

The girl finished her cheeseburger never considering whether her aunt was right or wrong. No one ever questioned Della. She wasn't going to be the first.

"Still don't know what to make of it. I guess we're having a wedding. Jimbo hasn't said we ain't. But it sure feels like we ain't moving toward a wedding. I don't know what to do. As long as Jimbo's spending time with Kathleen, he ain't going to be interested in me or a wedding. Not least ways marrying me." June rambled on as she cleaned her plate of ketchup with the last of her onion rings.

Goldie studied on what the young girl had to say. She put the pieces together like jigsaw puzzle but she was coming up short. Not wanting to jump to conclusions and influence June by anything she might say or suggestion, she spoke only to what the girl had shared leaving the rest to fall into place in its own timing.

"My best advice to you Junebug is to wait. Wait it out. Give the man the time he needs to make up his mind. If he loves you. He'll come to his senses. If he don't. Well, if he don't there ain't no amount of persuading that will change his mind. I think that's what your mama is telling you. You'll come closer to turning a mule than you will a man. You keep plowing your row straight. Marriage can wait. Pretty girl as yourself will be tripping over marriage proposals. Mark my words. You stop studying on getting married and start studying on something else and Jimbo will come around." Goldie said with conviction.

With her heart and mind as satisfied as her belly, June batted the threat of tears from her eyes and thanked Goldie for her advice knowing it was better than anything she would get from a year's worth of reading Seventeen magazine.

In need of an afternoon nap, Goldalena spent the time turning and tossing. The chocolate milk souring on her stomach and the images the young girl painted with her story of lost love and the waning admiration of a man she thought loved her enough to make her his bride. Her pillows felt like cistern blocks and the lightly starched cotton shirt felt heavy and itched her. Her bed sheets were cool when she got on the bed now damp from sweat. Goldie fought the pillows like she fought her thoughts. Trying to whip them both into submission but she couldn't manage neither. Like her thoughts the pillows mocked her. Surrendering to the ongoing battle she lay flat of the bed, her arms above her head and her legs reaching toward the outer corners of the foot of the bed. The grandfather clock ticked down the hall and water dripped in the kitchen sink. Just enough noise to distract her from what had been building for some time. Tomorrow marked the anniversary of her Henry's passing. She tried to keep herself busy but she couldn't out run her thoughts and the date on the calendar loomed like a dark cloud. Listening to June pine and whine over Jimbo stirred feelings in Goldie. Feelings she tried desperately to ignore. She would give her right arm to see Henry again. To lay awake like she was now and listen to him snore. And then tease him the following morning over fried eggs and bacon about the toast being burned because she couldn't sleep for his snoring. Reminding him if he ate biscuits like the rest of the south he wouldn't risk burned toast for breakfast. Only to hear him tell her every time that he liked the toast just the way she made it.

Burned and all. It was because she made it. Because she took the time to provide him with the things he enjoyed in life was what made waking up every day worth doing. Goldie wondered what she had to wake up to everyday for these last several years. She was grateful for her neighbors especially Florence and Ruskin Bright. If it hadn't been for them she would have ran from town like her hair was on fire. She wondered many times if they knew just how close she was to breaking into a hundred pieces and why it was the reason she wore Henry's clothes. Having him close, even if it was his clothes and the faint lingering scent of his aftershave buried deep into their fibers that kept her putting one foot in front of the other every day. Pulling his coat around her or pulling his pants up with his belt and wearing his socks gave her comfort beyond description. She knew she had to be a sight. But she didn't care. She figured if someone was brave enough to ask her why she was wearing her dead husband's clothes or tell her she shouldn't, then they could handle the tongue-lashing they were surely to get from being so bold. Today as she listened to June pour out her heart Goldie's already bruised and battered heart felt the loss fresh and new as if like tomorrow's anniversary, Henry had left her all over again. She understood the pain and loss. She understood it better than anyone. Maybe Kathleen Price understood too. Springing bolt right up in bed, Goldie knew what her next move would be. She would take time tomorrow between laying fresh flowers on Henry's grave, she would call on the young widow Kathleen Price and commiserate a spell.

Chapter Seventeen

oldie slows her Buick to a crawl. By the looks of the two houses, it would appear no one was at home. She admired the obvious hard work Virginia and Ellis had put in transforming the little sharecropper's house into a home. From the looks of the outside, all was going well on the inside. The cheerful yellow paint had faded slightly from its southern exposure but the flower bed brimming with tiger lilies and creeping flocks were enough to convince even the hardest of critiques that the two were trying to make the most out of what was given to them. Passing the tobacco field that separated two properties, its leafy crop reaching for the sky, Goldie's heart sank to see the house Kathleen and Sonny were calling home. Sad and forgotten it sat in the shadow of its neighbor.

The two ruts that passed as a driveway circled back toward the house from the road. If left to their own, they too would continue on to the warmer side of the holler. But, like most things on this side of the two properties, they faded into nothingness.

Goldie patted the Sweet William laying in the seat beside her. She had wrapped their tender roots with wet newspaper and knew if she visited too long they would soon wilt before she could get them transplanted at the cemetery. She open the car door and gave it a strong shove letting the door slam sending the message to the quiet house that someone had arrived.

Looking across the empty yard choked with Johnson grass, she studied the Chevy upon blocks and the scattering of tools laying on the ground at its raised hood. Realizing she had missed the person working on the car, the smell of fresh oil and rubber trailing from the car to her from the breeze floating through the holler. Not wanting to make a scene with Ellis and Virginia drawing conclusions of her visit, Goldie made her way to the house and on with her errand.

She knocked on the door standing ajar. She could hear

footsteps and the rattle of pans and water. She thought she heard someone humming but not expecting to find Kathleen in the best of spirits she dismissed the humming to something on the wind falling down through the hills off the ridge. Sound carries through these valleys and hollows making people unaccustomed to them to think the maker of the sound is right behind or just around the corner when they are miles away. It can be wonderful and haunting at the same time.

Knocking on the door and giving it a slight nudge, Goldie saw Kathleen rinsing out baby bottles in steaming water.

"Y'all already back. That was quick." Kathleen said, not turning around to see who had entered her home.

"You must be feeling a lot better. Up and around. Doing housework." Goldie said, standing in the doorway the door pushed open and the sun from the front yard trying to push through the porch's shadowy overhang.

"Morning Mrs. Filbry. This is a surprise."

"Goldie will be fine. Not wanting to surprise you. You looking fine. Feeling better are ye?"

"Better some. I have good days and bad days. And some days I can't tell the difference. Just have to enjoy the moments I have and wait for it all to pass. Least that's what everyone says."

"Good advice."

"Yes ma'am. What brings you out this way?"

"I was running over to the cemetery to put out some flowers on Henry's gravesite and thought I'd stop in and see you and the baby. Shame I've not gotten by here sooner but wanted to give you time."

"Whew, seems time is all I have these days. Can't seem to tell if I'm coming or going most days. Virginia has been coming in and helping me with Melody. You know she had a fever. Got that cleared up, thank the Lord. But, I'm just now getting on my feet good. Not sure what I'd done without Virginia and Ellis." Kathleen said, her attention drawn to the side window that overlooked the tobacco field and on to house next door.

"Good neighbors are hard to find. You got yourself two good ones that's for sure."

"Yes ma'am."

Kathleen lost in thought became embarrassed suddenly not certain what to do with the impromptu visitor. Goldie knowing she needed to get on with her purpose for dropping in helped herself to a chair nearest the door. The playpen pushed against the wall under the open window to it to catch the light and fresh air coming through the screen held a sleeping baby.

"She sure is a beauty. You and Sonny must be very proud. I know it had to be a scare when she took sick but she looks right as rain now. Well, it won't be long she will be running these hills and hollers like you young'uns did not too long ago." Goldie said.

"I can only hope Sonny will be back to see it." Kathleen said, tossing her cup towel over her shoulder, drying her hands on her apron and joining Goldie in an adjacent chair. She too looked into the playpen and admired her sleeping daughter.

"Back. What do you mean back? I thought Sonny passed in the car crash."

"No ma'am. Least not as we know it for certain."

"Oh I see. Well, honey I guess it's good to hope for the best but you can't expect to have him just walk up one day just out of the blue like he never left. From what I understand, that was a terrible wreck. No one could have survived that fire. If he did, don't you think he would have needed to go the hospital least ways a doctor?"

"Sonny knew those roads like the back of his hand. Manys a time he talked about all a body needed to do was know how and when to jump if and when they were going off the side. I've lost count the number of times we've gone to town and back and all the way there and back listening to him tell of how all anyone needed to do was know when to jump. Scares me now just thinking about it."

"You're telling me you think he jumped? Jumped from the car before it went over the edge."

"Yes ma'am. He talked about it enough he had us all convinced he could do it in his sleep."

"I've never heard such."

"That's Sonny Price for you. A born daredevil. If it's something that can't be done be sure he's tried it and proved it can. That's why I believe he'll be back. That and Virginia has seen him."

"Seen him. Seen him since the car crash."

"Yes ma'am. I guess it was about a month or two afterwards. I was still feeling poorly and she was here watching over me and the baby. Said she couldn't sleep. It was a full moon and the window curtains there were just too thin to keep out the light. Said she was up giving the baby her bottle and couldn't go back to sleep cause of the light so she just stayed up. That's when she saw him. Least that's who she thinks it was. Could have been a coon hunter or just shadows is what Ellis told her but Virginia wouldn't have none of it. Said there were no dogs out so that took care of the coon hunter idea and no one else would have need or reason to be cutting across that field 'cept it was Sonny come check on things. Virginia was convinced and I got to tell you she had me convinced of it too. Can't say the same for Ellis but Ellis has a mind of his own and just like every other man exercises it when he chooses."

"Well, ain't that something. So you reckon he was come to check on you and the baby?"

"Yes ma'am. Wouldn't put it past him to have come by here since then too. Sort of makes me feel comforted to know he ain't too far from home. Guess he'll make his way back when he's good and ready. I think that's what Jimbo expects too."

"Jimbo. Jimbo's been out here asking questions?" Goldie asked trying to keep up with revelations.

"He's out here regularly. I 'spect to seem him today. Comes most times after dinner but can't say that's his schedule or anything. He just shows up. Comes to the door or walks up if I'm outside, asks me the same question every time. When was the last time you saw Sonny. I tell him the same thing every time. I don't remember cause of the baby blues. And he asks if he can walk around and take a look. I say yes every time. And every time he walks from here to out past the garden and the 'bacco field, circles around past Ellis and Virginia's and then back up the road. Gets in his car and drives off waving like he was here for Sunday dinner."

"And you don't mind? You don't find that odd?"

"Not Jimbo. I figure he's doing his job. Sheriff Bright can't 'spect to be everywhere at once and Jimbo and me go way back. We courted before Sonny and me got married. Guess it would hurt Sonny's feelings something awful if he knew it was Jimbo coming around here checking on things. But there ain't nothing between us. Never was. Least not for me. That's why I married Sonny. Married for love. That's the only way."

"Love. Yep. That's the only way. So you say he comes out here regular like. Don't offer up anything other than asking you when was the last time you saw Sonny and then take a look around."

"Yes ma'am. That's it. Ellis says they ain't got nothing on Sonny. Nothing to keep him. If and when Sonny decides to show up things will go right back to the way they were. Like he never left."

"What do you mean? You mean Ellis don't plan to press charges about the car."

"That's what I mean."

"Sounds like y'all got it all figured out."

"I don't know Miss Goldie. Some days I think I do. I think I'll be piddle around here and he'll come through that door just like he never left. And, we'll take up right where we left off. But then there are days, when I think we are just trying catch smoke. That he wasn't as clever as he thought he was or we thought he was and he really did die in that crash and they just ain't had time to find his remains." Kathleen said.

Goldie sat quietly deep in her own thoughts and reflections trying to piece together everything that had been said to her. Kathleen's mind raced with details and as she poured out the story and her heart and then replaying it all in her mind. She remembered one thing she had left out.

"Jimbo did say one thing. I just remembered it now that we've been talking about it. Guess it was early on when he was first coming around. That's been some time now when I think back on it. Anyway, he was explaining why he was here. Guess it must have been the first couple of times but I think he only said this once. Not sure why I forgot it seems like something important to remember." Kathleen said, her face shining with promise at the rush of memory coming to the surface.

Goldie sat on the edge of the chair waiting for Kathleen to stop rambling and spit it out. Her frustration building making her want to reach in and pull the words out herself and be on to her errand.

"He said that the fire burned so long and so hot that if there had been anyone in the car their remains would be burned to dust."

A cold chill ran over Goldie's body like someone had walked over her grave. How could that bring such enthusiasm to Kathleen? She all but beamed with excitement. Goldie suddenly felt like she was caught in a snare. She had hung on every word believing what her eyes were seeing, a young healthy woman with no obvious ailment but it was clear to her now, Kathleen's mind had snapped some time ago and she was actually sitting across from a crazy woman.

For the last hour she had spent time listening to her weave a story with such conviction that Goldie began to believe it herself. Like sitting in the pew at church, listening to the preacher recount the familiar stories she had heard her whole life but hearing them for the first time every time, she was ready to accept what Kathleen was saying. But now, that she was certain that if her husband had not jumped from the car as he had insisted for years was the way to escape any car accident on the steep roads of the ridge with their ravines dropping for miles below, she was comforted by the news that his young body once full of life and promise would have disintegrated to unrecognizable ashes, was more than Goldie could handle. Especially with her Henry only around the bend in the road, laying in his eternal rest, how could this young woman be mourning with such relief to believe her husband of a few years and courtship had died a horrific death?

Kathleen finished her thought with no thought to how

her expression of relief sounded. "To know he could have died in the fire is to know he didn't suffer."

Goldie swallowed hard unable to force the images and words down as Kathleen continued to explain. "If I thought he hadn't jumped. If he'd somehow went off the ridge and ended up at the bottom and got out of the car before it went up in flames or if he was somehow thrown from the car, hurt and mangled, unable to care for himself and eventually dying cold and alone in the woods or if by chance someone came upon and took him in not knowing who he was because he was so disfigured, I just couldn't live. Don't you see? Don't you see the great burden that would be to live a life with that running through my mind and heart forever? Trust me. I know my husband. If he said he could jump. He jumped."

Grief does strange things to people. If anyone understood that it would be Goldalena Filbry. Wearing her husband's clothes for a decade or more would be more than enough to send her to a padded room at Clover Bottom for the rest of her natural life so to sit in judgment of Kathleen's rationalization of what did or didn't happen to her dead husband was inexcusable. Goldie had more in common with Kathleen than she cared to admit.

Goldie had heard enough. If she was going to make it out to the cemetery before the roots dried out on her flowers she needed to go now. Saying her goodbyes and asking for the pardon of just dropping in she made her way to the door only to have Kathleen offer to go with her to the cemetery. To repay the favor of company. She too understood the loss. Whether Sonny was dead or alive, she was alone and new the weight of it. She had no guarantees he would ever come back if he was alive and was already considered a widow by most. She didn't want to disrespect Goldie but wanted to show respect by going with her to help plant the flowers. Goldie was grateful for the company and the two drove off with little Melody riding along across her mother's lap.

Chapter Eighteen

Virginia watched as the Buick made its way down the road. Out from Kathleen's house, around the bend and out of sight. Curiosity was eating a hole in her brain. She didn't know what business the widow Filbry had with Kathleen. She had eavesdropped on a conversation between two of her sisters-in-law on the party line that Goldalena Filbry and Florence Bright had been to Della's. She suspected her sisters-in-law knew someone was on the line listening. They just didn't know it was her. It would seem the woman is making herself familiar lately. Showing up at Della's and now at Kathleen's. What interest she had in their family business was soon to be Virginia's business too. She saw Kathleen in the passenger side of the car. And, she was almost certain it looked like they were in deep conversation about whatever they had been visiting about since they came out of the house talking and were still talking when the car went by Virginia's. Fortunate for Virginia and her need to keep an eye on all things concerning Kathleen, especially now that Sonny was gone, although she had plenty of practice before he left, she had an excellent view from her bedroom window of the goings on at Kathleen's. And when the light was just right, like it was today, and when Kathleen kept her curtains pulled back, like they were today, Virginia could see straight through Kathleen's bedroom window into the front room. That's where she saw Goldie Filbry and Kathleen talking for the last hour or so and now they have gone off down the road together. Just as Virginia was getting ready to step out onto her front porch to get a better look down the road she heard a car door slam. Knowing it was impossible for Goldie and Kathleen to have come back by without her seeing, she knew it couldn't be them returning so soon. Following her curiosity she stepped out onto the porch and looked toward Kathleen and Sonny's place as was her habit.

Cutting across the tobacco field instead of taking the long way around going behind it between the log road and the cow pasture or taking the road over to the Kathleen and Sonny's, Virginia was a few steps away from stepping out of the lush field of tobacco and onto the withering rye grass of the little yard. She saw Jimbo long before he saw her and feeling the need to act offended at his lack of respect for their privacy helping himself to look around not knowing if anyone was at home, Virginia made her presence known.

"You looking for something in particular there Deputy?" Virginia said, stepping upon the front porch with a stomp.

Startled Jimbo turned quickly almost losing his footing on the narrow porch in serious need of repair. "Hey there Virginia. I didn't see you come up. How you and Ellis getting along?"

"How are we getting along? What are you trying to insinuate Jimbo? You know something I don't? You got something you want to tell me?"

"Heck no Virginia. Calm down. I was just..."

"Calm down. I think you're the one that needs to calm down. Showing up here. Helping yourself to private property. What you hoping to find? You think Kathleen is sitting around here pining after a man? You think she is waiting on you to show up and save the day?"

"Good God in Heaven Virginia what has gotten into you? I've never seen you like this. You know full well what I'm doing here. I've been coming by here for going on six maybe seven months checking on things. Ever since Ellis said..."

"Ellis? Just what did my husband say?"

Jimbo uncertain that Ellis had shared with his wife that he had confided in him that she had seen Sonny return home in the middle of the night and that rumors were spreading in town about someone scrounging around in the middle of the night. He knew that Goldie Filbry had someone take things from her cellar and others had similar suspicions but no one but Virginia had seen him since the accident. It was Ruskin's hope that if Jimbo could intercept Sonny on one of his nightly runs that he could explain to him that no charges were pending. He could come home. That is, if he wanted to come home. And, if it wasn't

Sonny, then the town had bigger problems.

Looking around and not seeing Kathleen home and nothing appearing to be any different than his last visit a week earlier, Jimbo decided to leave well enough alone with Virginia Hatch and call it a day.

Tipping his hat, he stepped off the porch and began making his way back to his patrol car with Virginia staring holes in the back of his head all the way.

"You didn't answer my question Deputy Bishop. You going to answer me or just run off? Is that what all you men do when things don't go to your liking?"

Jimbo kept walking as if he were fleeing from any other predatory animal ready to pounce at the slightest sign of fear. Keeping his eyes forward, his head down and his feet moving slow and steady he got in the police car and drove off as if she was not standing there waiting for his answer.

All the way down the ridge, as his heart returned beating at its normal pace, he prayed a silent prayer for Ellis Hatch.

* * *

Goldie pulled the Buick into the cemetery and followed the narrow gravel road up and around to where Henry lay near the cedar thicket. Home to bees and dirt daubers Goldie hated that thicket and threatened to move their plots to a different location if he should go before her. But things said in haste are rarely remembered or acted upon when their time for action is upon us and the last thing Goldie thought of doing the day they laid her Henry to his final rest was her complaining about the trees. But now as she fought for space among the stinging insects, she regretted not being in more control of her senses at that time.

Kathleen asked if she wanted her and the baby to wait in the car but Goldie said it was silly to not get out and at least stretch her legs. Kathleen knew the two mile drive around the bend and upon Shy's Hill was not long enough for anyone needing to stretch their legs but she didn't want to upset Goldie.

She looked around for familiar names. Seeing many that

she recognized she thought of how different her life would be right now if it was her that was bringing flowers to her husband's grave. If it was her routine to come visit his last place on this earth and if she could bring herself to maintain such a ritual. Once again she thanked God for keeping Sonny safe wherever he may be and asked too that whatever was keeping him away would soon be reconciled. She trusted God to hear her prayers even when she had no idea what the expected outcome would look like. She just had to pray and believe and leave the rest to God. It was as simple and as complicated as that.

"That's a pretty stone." Kathleen said kneeling down beside Goldie. She put the baby between them as a buffer. They both were lost in their own revere and it seemed natural to have a reminder of things of this world. The baby with her little coos and lips dripping with slobber kept them anchored to the place in spite of their wanting to be where their husbands were.

"Thank you. I think Henry would be proud of it. Decided to put just the one here. Didn't seem right leaving that big empty space next to his name just waiting to carve mine in it. Folks do it all the time I know but it just seemed wrong at the time. I wanted it to be just about Henry. Not me. I wanted to honor Henry. Best way I thought I could do that was have no trace of me here. Guess that may be why I took to wearing his clothes. Came home from laying him out here, took off my black dress and put on his black suit. Slept in it that night. Just felt right. Like he was there with me. Not here. Couldn't bring myself to wear anything of mine after that. One day slipped into the next and before I knew it I was wearing his clothes and folks just going right along with me. Not saying a word." Goldie paused as if rewinding the scenes playing out in her mind. "Folks have a way of leaving you to your grief. They do their best to say the right thing or at least not say the wrong thing but by and by the best thing folks do is just leave you to it. Guess I never thought of it until now. It helps. I can say it sure has helped me."

The baby pulled at the grass between her chubby bare legs and watched as a black ant crawled over her knee. Kathleen wiped the ant away and wiped away a tear from her eye before it fell announcing itself. She felt guilty for being thankful she wasn't there spreading flowers on her husband's grave. Her heart broke fresh for Goldie and the heavy load she had been carrying. She admired the old woman's spunk and wanted to be like that at that age but with it came a deep well of emotion that Kathleen feared. She didn't want to know the loss that Goldie faced every day. She knew Sonny was gone and she wanted to hold on to the hope that he would come back. If not, she knew her only hope was to someday be spreading flowers on his grave while their daughter thought of the man she loved and missed.

"If you're right about your man, you've postponed this misery for a while." Goldie said causing Kathleen to burn with embarrassment.

"I was just thinking that." Kathleen said her voice cracking with emotion. Guilt, shame and longing for Sonny to walk up right now and prove her right flooded her and she began to tremble.

"Those Hatch sisters must agree with you. That's for sure." Goldie said sensing the conversation needed to take a turn.

"What do you mean?"

"Oh nothing I'm sure I was just imagining it but Florence Bright, you know Florence, Sheriff Bright's wife, my neighbor, we were over by Della's. They were filling their stamp books and something got said about Sonny. For the life of me I can't remember exactly what got said or by who. This is when we need Florence. That woman's brain is like a steel trap. She'd remember. Anyway, something was said and I don't know which sister got bowed up first but it was like dominoes. They all got stirred up and commenced to talking at the same time. Can't say I remember exactly what was said but I do know it was about Sonny. Left me believing the sisters don't believe he's dead or if they do they don't think too kindly to Jimbo Bishop coming around visiting the way he is. Now that got me to thinking, what would Jimbo Bishop be doing coming around her place if he is getting ready to marry June. Guess those old hens got their feathers ruffled for more than one reason."

Knowing the visit at Della's didn't go exactly the way she was remembering it. Goldie waited to see what Kathleen's reaction would be to hearing how others were thinking about her situation.

"I don't care what those old bats have to say about anything. Whether Sonny is dead or alive is none of their business. Best thing for them is for him to walk right in and show them all that he is alive and well. That'll stop their tongues from wagging."

Goldie laughed, "Ah honey, won't nothing stop a gossip from talking. If they are talking about you they're giving someone else a rest. You just don't never mind what they have to say. You don't answer to them."

Kathleen pulled the baby to her for comfort and support. Speaking to the baby as though it was the baby that had started the conversation, "We just have to wait it out. That's all."

"Well that sounds like good and sound advice. You listen to your mama little one. You just need to wait it out. Things work out in the end." Smoothing out the grass on the plot, Goldie spoke to the ground as though speaking to Henry, "They always do."

* * *

Feeling especially satisfied with herself over getting Jimbo Bishop riled up, Virginia sat on her front porch and ate a Popsicle watching and waiting for the Buick to round the bend. She wasn't sure what she would do when she saw it. Not certain she wanted to be neighborly and throw up her hand to say hello as if she expected Kathleen to have interests she wasn't aware of and that those secret interests involved Goldie Filbry and taking drives in the middle of the day in Goldie's Buick to only God knows where. She didn't want to get up and leave the porch either when she saw the car and risk them seeing her leaving, turning her back on them and the secret fun they've been having or to not be seen and they never knowing she knew about the little ride in the car. She knew she would do the right thing whatever it was. She always did. Even when she didn't know what the right thing to do was or if she didn't know it was the right thing at the time she knew she could explain things in such a way that everyone would be convinced that once again Virginia did the right thing.

She saw the roiling dirt cloud long before she saw the Buick. The brown cloud of dust lifting above the treetops and spreading out thin under the clear blue sky. She had no guarantee it was them but she couldn't risk it not being them. The Popsicle had done its trick and cooled her dry throat but left a sticky sweetness in her mouth that begged for water. Judging the distance of the cloud of road dust she figured she could get inside, get a drink of water to wash out the residue and be back out on the porch waiting leisurely looking like she was waiting for the day to pass and not the Buick but she was wrong. Just as she swallowed the water, she saw the Buick sail by the front of the house with its occupants laughing inside from something she didn't get to hear. It felt like they were laughing at her.

Jealousy swelled in Virginia from a deep recess that broke open from an old scab. Searing contempt spread throughout her body leaving her furious at its original source and the one that caused the pain now. She was caught in the middle and needed to find a way out.

Chapter Nineteen

Virginia lay in the warm bed drinking in the lingering smell of her husband's body. She rolled on her side and watched as Ellis passed the bedroom window working the hard packed dirt from the summer shower. The window screen matched the rhythm of her breathing moving in and out. The morning warming to a promising day.

Try as she might, Virginia couldn't push down the chill that swam through her bones. The chill that flooded her at the beginning of the year. She tried to ignore it. Sometimes that worked. But there were days when ignoring wasn't enough. She told herself lies but just as she assumed she wasn't a very good liar even to herself.

The voices. The voices full of raw emotion played like a scratched record in her head skipping when the needle got caught playing and replaying the words that she couldn't drown out.

She had promised Ellis on their wedding night that she would keep the secret. A family secret that now that she was a member of the family it was her duty as well to know and hold its truth deep inside and never under any circumstances let it be known.

Thinking back to how careful Ellis was unfolding this family mystery to her and how easy it was for her to accept such a heavy responsibility, she considered that maybe it took her, an outsider, to appreciate the fact that it truly wasn't as dangerous as Ellis and his sisters thought, and maybe just maybe, it took someone like her, a level headed person to expose the truth. To set it free.

Just when she thought she had convinced herself that she was the secret keepers' rescuer, she would see the faces of her brothers-in-law, stern faces creased with a lifetime of wisdom and untold truths. It was then she knew she was no one's rescuer. She was nothing more than a gossip. An emotional woman that let circumstances get the best of her. When her family needed her the most, she let them down by exposing the one they held the dearest. And, the one thing that would forever change his life.

"Words are givers and takers of life." She could hear mother-in-law say. *"Be careful which ones you give away because you can't get them back."* Virginia loved her in-laws and missed them dearly. Part of her was thankful they were no longer alive to know the damage she had done. She was, for the first time, thankful for their departing. Theirs and Olive Price's passing too. A precious triangle of friendship and love that now because of her, would forever be judged in the harshest of light.

Virginia sat up on the edge of the bed. Again she drank in the sweet smell of flowers opening to the morning's warmth and tried to free her mind of the argument. But Sonny's voice, her voice, and the looks from the emergency room nurse, who heard it all, were as real as if they were all in the room with her.

She had tried to comfort Sonny. Explain that Kathleen was going to be alright. That she hadn't lost her mind. That the sadness would pass. It was common. Just baby blues. But Sonny lashed back. Reminding Virginia that she had no way of knowing such things. She'd never know. She hadn't carried a baby. Hadn't birthed one. She had no idea of any of the things she was saying. She was just talking. Like she always did. Like some know-it all that grew up in town, read too many books, and thought she was better than everybody else.

Virginia's body jerked as she sat on the edge of the bed, just like it did that morning in the emergency room waiting area, with each insult a blow to what she believed about herself but didn't know anyone else held the same opinion. Now she knew. She knew everyone thought the worst of her and the emergency room nurse, with her snow white uniform starched and pressed without a smudge or wrinkle adding insult to injury with her smirking exposing her eavesdropping.

Virginia tried her best to keep her mouth shut. To let Sonny run off at the mouth like he was known to do. She watched him pace the floor like a caged animal. She tried to put herself in his shoes. Too immature to be a father and too inexperienced to figure out a way to accept the responsibility. She knew it was more than even the most seasoned of men could handle. She wanted to be sympathetic to Sonny. She wanted to love him like Ellis and the sisters did but she couldn't. Not in that moment when he ripped the skin from her flesh opening her up to ridicule and shame. If anyone should know the pain of shame it should be Sonny Price.

The words were out of her mouth before she heard them in her ears. Like trying to hear underwater, she wasn't sure she said anything until she saw the look on Sonny's face. The look that has haunted her for months. Out of the corner of her eye, she saw too that the nurse caught up in the live drama playing out in front of her, no longer hid behind her receptionist desk, but like an animal caught in a trap, she too was stunned by Virginia's revelation.

Virginia watched as the effect worked its way down Sonny's trembling body. Once vibrating with fear of the unknown for his feverish daughter, now quaked at the unyielding blow from the person he thought was his best-friend's wife, his neighbor in good times and bad, who now removed all doubt of the rumors that had followed him through life. A life spent running from the rumors.

Virginia couldn't stop the rush of words once they began coming. Like a warm weather spring, bursting out of the soft earth, the facts of Sonny's parentage spilled out onto the emergency room floor and rose like floodwaters drowning him in disbelief.

Even now as Virginia grips the moist sheets under her sweating palms, she can taste the bitterness in her mouth from the freed secret and see the disgust in the eyes of the interloping nurse. She could still see how Sonny's knees buckled a time or two and his eyes appeared to be seeing things far off instead of Virginia sitting bowed upright in the plastic chair of the waiting room twisting and twitching with apparent delight with each revelation.

Virginia had spread his life out in front of him like Ralph Edwards on This is Your Life. Everything mocked him. Every moment in his life suddenly felt like a lie. He wanted to escape.

Run from the truth. Run from the lie. Run as far away from everyone and everything that resembled the life he no longer trusted.

As Virginia's mouth kept moving, dishing out dirt on the people he thought he knew. Her tongue appearing to savor each word. Sonny remembered the car parked just outside the doors. He remembered Ellis's habit of leaving the keys in the ignition. He could hear Ellis joking about no one wanting to steal a rattletrap and how his old clunker was the safest car in town. Sonny pushed through the weight that forced him to stand and listen. He pushed through the doors and stepped out into the cold letting it fold around him and stop the rushing undertow Virginia had stirred up threatening to pull him under and drown him.

His mind was frozen with rage. He didn't know who he was angry with but the emotion driving the car was in complete control. It whispered to him telling him he didn't have to listen. He knew who he was and Virginia had no right saying different. He had every right to be angry. He had the right to expect his father to be the man he believed him to be. And, he had the right to love the woman he called his mother.

The car maneuvered the ice-covered roads with ease. Sonny marveled at how well he managed the slick streets and decided to open up the engine on the ridge. He felt fearless. He had nothing to lose. Everything he knew to be his life had been ripped from him in one careless moment. He was alone in this world. A place he no longer recognized.

The old Chevy topped the first hill of the rising foothills. Its motor whining for more. Giving it more gas and accelerating down the incline to catch the next rise with even more speed, Sonny ignored the warnings rising up from the pits of his stomach. He told himself it was just the feeling of his stomach dropping out with each dip and dive but he knew it was real. He knew he was going too fast on the ice especially at that time of day. Deer were known to cross in the early morning and many times truck drivers trying to make their destination in the last few fleeting minutes of their route had plowed into a doe crossing the road its mangled body left on the roadside as a reminder to other travelers.

But Sonny felt fearless. He felt like he could fly. Like everything that he thought was possible, everything he had boasted about growing up, was suddenly there for him to prove it could be done. He was tired of talking about it. He was ready to live it.

It was in that moment of realization. When he decided he had lived too long in the shadows of good intentions and crippling doubt, the car topped the highest ridge's highest peak, rounded the hairpin curve and hit a deer.

As if an unseen force opened the car door for him, Sonny instinctively rolled out of the car from behind the wheel and landed in a rhododendron thicket just off the shoulder. He lay there listening. He could hear the car when it left the road. The sound of the trees snapping and breaking from the car plowing down the ravine. The scrap of metal against stone knowing the car had struck an outcropping of limestone that swelled up from the ground throughout the county. His mind's eye could see the sparks and in the span of two heartbeats he heard the explosion. The rumble of fire and the popping of rubber hoses and belts melting in the heat growing in intensity. Somewhere near him, he heard the faint sound of the deer's last breath as her torment ended with the crescendo of the explosion.

All of this played out just a few yards in front of him on the opposite side of the road. He knew it wouldn't be long before someone would hear the explosion, or spot the rising cloud of black smoke over the tree line, and call the authorities. He thought about staying put and call out to whoever was the first on the scene. But after taking a quick inventory of his injuries and the nagging feeling that he couldn't go back to the way things were, the need to run rekindled in his gut and using the evergreen bush to pull himself to a standing position waiting until his feet agreed and then he took off walking.

Chapter Twenty

Jimbo honked the horn of his pickup truck. Virginia looked out the window. She saw Ellis pull up on the reins bringing the mule to a stop. She watched as he wiped his brow with the back of his arm smearing more sweat than removing it. She knew Jimbo could see her standing in the parted curtains but he never made any indication of speaking to her keeping his eyes trained on Ellis.

Ellis took a dip of water from the water bucket sitting in the tall grass at the corner of the field, tossed the last sip from the dipper before returning it to the bucket. He called out to Jimbo and joined him at the pickup.

Both men leaned against the truck, their feet crossed in front of them, each looking out at an arbitrary spot just in front of them in the mix of loose gravel and dirt that was the make shift driveway and then at each other depending on who was speaking. Virginia strained to hear what was being said but the breeze was blowing up from the south carrying their words with it and away from her prying ears. Neither appeared to care whether she was standing at the window watching but something in the way their backs were pressed against the truck and the small gap of space between them caused her to reconsider more than once about leaving the window and joining them.

Guilt had plagued her all morning and as dinner time approached and she didn't have anything on the table for Ellis to eat, she knew her time was better spent rushing to get food on the table and not trying to piece together what business those two had with one another.

Twice she tried to turn to the kitchen and twice she failed. Her curiosity was too great and it overpowered her. Virginia knew she would soon pay for telling Sonny the secret. She knew it would catch up with her soon enough. She had prayed many nights that Sonny had died in the crash. It would solve all of her problems. Her mishap would die with him. But then conviction would take hold and she would spend the rest of the night praying for forgiveness. Her prayers a tangled mess of contrition and fear not knowing exactly what she was asking forgiveness for and being met with a silence that felting like shouting.

In all of her living and reliving the events of that dreadful morning, she had forgotten the eavesdropping nurse. She didn't know her and dismissed her as soon as her mind was able to erase her from her memory. But what Virginia didn't know then and was about to find out was the nurse knew her.

That was what Jimbo had come to tell Ellis. As Ellis waited for Jimbo to drive off, watching his truck fade out of sight around and up the hill from their house, as he stood in yard just off from the porch where Virginia waited for him to say something, his eyes a mix of anger and disappointment, he opened and closed his mouth like a fish out of water gasping for air but nothing, no sound came out. Virginia wanted to say something to end the suspense. She knew like she knew everything else what Ellis was trying to say but the words wouldn't form in his mouth. She hoped it was love for her that had muted him but fear and dread tapped down any hope she had of him seeing beyond her mistake through loving eyes and without hesitation forgive her. The pain on her husband's face was unbearable but she knew it was only a matter of time and he would be calm enough to find the words. Words she dreaded.

She watched as he took one step after another as if suddenly carrying a weight too heavy for his back, and returned to his plowing. She wanted to sink down through the cracks in the wooden porch. Slip through the part in the boards and seep into the worm infested ground. That's where she belonged. Down deep where light couldn't penetrate. Where filth germinated and decay spread. But not enough wishing could remove her from the inevitable. Ellis couldn't plow forever. The field was only just so big and the mule only just so willing. Ellis would find the time and the hour and Virginia would just have to wait.

Chapter Twenty-one

Turning out onto the highway that came down from the state line, ran through the middle of Fulton, coiled around Scots Ridge and dipped through Tillman on its way to the opposite state line, Goldie prayed silently. Rolling down the windows and sliding open the vents at their feet, the car cooled off making the ride more comfortable.

"Where we going? If you don't mind me asking." June asked.

"Thought we'd take a turn out by Kathleen Price's." Goldie said.

June wanted to jump. Looking at her hand gripping the car door handle she wondered if the stories were true about Sonny jumping from the car. She wondered just how easy something like that would be. Could she do it too? Would she survive? Goldie appeared to ignore the sudden shift in June and kept driving towards the ridge. June knew she had to do something. Say something before they left Tillman and headed up the ridge. She had to come up with some reason why she couldn't possibly go to Kathleen's. What if Jimbo showed up while she was there? What would she do? What would she say? And, then there's Kathleen. How could she possibly be polite to the one woman that was causing her such heartache? Whether her suspicions were true or not about Kathleen and Jimbo picking up where they left off, she had spent too many sleepless nights thinking about it and there was no way to undo those thoughts between here and Mud Flats. She had to say something to make Goldie reconsider.

"I can't." That was all June could manage and she doubted Goldie heard her over the wind plowing through the car.

"Can't? Can't what?"

"I just can't go to Kathleen's. I'm sorry. Maybe you can let me out somewhere along the way and pick me up on your way back." June winced as sweat rolled across the razor burn in her armpits.

"Don't be silly. I'm not going to drop you anywhere. What do you got against Kathleen?" Goldie said.

June was almost in tears. How could Goldie be so blind to what was going on? Had she not explained enough about Jimbo to her that she shouldn't have to say more? Couldn't Goldie put two and two together? June sat quietly. Shaking her head, forcing back tears, she refused to try to explain. It was all too much too fast.

"Kathleen did me a favor the other day and I want to thank her for it. Made her some fried pies." Goldie said glancing back to the grease stained brown paper bag in the backseat. It was sitting on a piece of newspaper spread out to keep the bacon fat from seeping through the paper sack and onto the seat cushion. It was one of many ways Goldie used the newspapers she saved from week to week.

"What'd she do?" June said. Her voice breaking with emotion.

"Nothing she would take any credit for, or that I'd ever mention to her. But kindness goes a long way in this life. And, it'll be a good thing to remember."

June swallowed hard digesting the admonition and the sweet aroma of fried bread and peaches that now filled her senses as wind cycled through the car's open windows. She hoped Kathleen was as gracious with the fried pies as she was with her time and offered her one or two. June could taste them as her mouth watered the closer they got to where Kathleen and Sonny lived in the hollow at the bottom of Shepherd's Gap.

Bracing herself for whatever would come of this impromptu visit and not sure how she would manage being polite and not look like some silly school girl with a boy-crazy crush instead of a grown woman engaged to a man. A man they both wanted. June felt light-headed and weak-kneed. She told herself it was the fried pies and not fear but she knew it was more fear than hunger.

Just as the car rounded the last turn and the road narrowed to gravel, Goldie turned into a pasture opening and stopped the car at the cattle gate. Turning off the ignition she adjusted in the seat to look and speak squarely at June. "I don't know what notions you have going on in your head about Kathleen and Jimbo."

June started to speak but the expression on Goldie's face was enough to render her mute.

"Hear me out." Goldie said. "I don't know what you've heard and I don't need to know. June, you can spend your life running from this one to that one asking for advice or getting it whether you ask or not. Folks are going to talk. It's just that simple. You've got to make your mind up sooner rather than later about what you are going to believe. It's been my experience to trust myself first and not the opinion of others. No one knows how you feel but you. You love Jimbo and he loves you. That's enough. That's all you need."

June started again to interrupt.

"I know. You think because he is coming up here that he is somehow back stepping and stirring up old feelings. Girl, you can't confuse duty with love. Too many folks have spent their whole lives doing that and I'm telling you now, if you don't hear another word I say, that's the reason we're all in this mess, but that's all I'll say on it. Jimbo has a job to do and that's all he is doing. Don't turn it into something it ain't and don't let anyone make you believe otherwise."

June nodded. Her face flush from the heat mounting in the car and from the well of emotions flooding her body.

Goldie pulled the gear shift down into reverse, backed the car out onto the gravel road and slowly drove the small stretch of road up to the two small houses on the back side of Ephraim Hatch's farm. Nestled behind a well maintained yard with its rich bluegrass and old tractor tires painted white transformed into flower beds, the once yellow now faded to cream clapboard house boasted a metal "H" on its screen door. Rolling by the house and the tobacco field, Goldie slowed to give June an extra few minutes to collect herself.

"Looks like Ellis and Virginia have taken off to enjoy this nice weather." Goldie said not expecting a response just thinking out loud. Her tone was strained like she was making an extra effort to sound more pleasant than she had been. She knew she could have said things differently to June. But, just like a pressure cooker building steam, Goldie had built up a head of steam and it was only a matter of time before someone caught the brunt of it. She knew too that it would do June good to heed her warning and not get too caught up in how it was said.

"Probably around at the cemetery. Mama said something the other day about Virginia taking to caring for the family plots over there. 'Specially Pa's and Granny's. Said she never was one to spend too much time there less it was Decoration Day and there was a meal to be had after the work but now seems like she's there more often than not. I don't know how Mama knows this but you know my mama. She knows things others only wonder." June said looking out across the tobacco field that separates the two houses. She tried to imagine Sonny running across it with the small pink bundle laying across his arms, his body becoming as feverish as the baby's, and the ice cracking under his feet and raining down on him from the sky. She remembered her daddy being one of the ones that let out that day to look for Sonny and how he wasn't gone an hour or two before the freezing rain sent everyone back to their homes to give up the search until the weather cleared. Fear and concern for Sonny surviving the crash and laying injured or dying gave way to their own personal safety and health. No one believed he survived the fiery crash. June's daddy being one to say it aloud when others only thought about it.

"I don't reckon anyone's at home. A pretty day like today I guess I can't fault a body for wanting to get out and enjoy it. I'm going to run these pies up to the door and you can sit here or step out and stretch your legs." Goldie put the car in gear and didn't worry setting the emergency brake finding the only level spot in the rutted out dirt to park the car without fear of it rolling back down into the road. The bank of grass that led up from the road was ankle high and she thought of the effort it would take to mow it. It tired her just thinking about pushing a mower up and down that embankment. It made her thankful for living in town and on her level lot. Small as it was. It was hers and she could manage it. Even in death, Judge Filbry was still a protector.

"Hello in the house." Goldie called out as she knocked on the front door and peeked into the window of the front room. The room looked just like she remembered it not a thing out of place or moved since her last visit. It almost had the look as though Kathleen had not been there since but she knew better. Where else could the woman go? With no family of her own to shake a stick at, none she ever would lean on in times of trouble or rejoicing, Kathleen Price and her baby girl were alone in this world.

"Anyone there?" June asked stepping upon the porch and cupping her hands around her eyes to see into the window through the threadbare curtains.

"Nope. Just as I figured. She's gone off for the day."

"You gonna just leave that bag sitting here? Anything could help itself to it."

"Hadn't thought of that. No use going to all this trouble to feed a rat. I'm feeding enough of those in town."

"What. How are you feeding rats in town?" June said second guessing her decision to move in with the widow.

"My cellar. Something or somebody has been helping itself to my cellar."

June watched as the color changed in Goldie's face as she stirred herself up with the thoughts of someone stealing from her.

"I know what you mean. Mama said she heard at the A&P the other day that couple of our neighbors had things missing from their places. Daddy told her not to pay too much attention to the things people say standing in the check out at the grocery store but Mama said it had to be true because Brother Strap from over at the Baptist church was one of the ones doing the talking. I guess it was enough to convince Daddy there must be some truth to it because he didn't say no more. And now that I think about it, Mama didn't either." June winced fearing she had said too much about her parents and their bickering.

"Well, I hate it. Just hate it for us all. Got enough going on around us with young boys being called up on the draft and hooligans like this one here running off leaving his wife to fend for herself. These are sad times. You only have to pick up a newspaper or watch it on the television. I sure hoped Scots Ridge, Fulton and Tillman would stay safe and free from the troubles but I'm beginning to have my doubts." Goldie sat down in the shade of the porch and opened the bag offering a fried pie to June and ate one too.

June saddled up beside the widow leaving enough space for personal comfort and the breeze to pass between them. She chewed her fried pie slowly not knowing if another would be offered and said. "You don't think whoever this is prowling around is from somewhere other than Scots Ridge do you?"

"I don't rightly know. Does it make it easier to accept that someone so desperate to steal is willing to steal from people he knows instead of strangers? I'm telling you Junebug it hurts my head just thinking about it." Goldie said swallowing the last bite of peach and fried dough before reaching into the bag and drawing out another for herself and June.

June accepted the second pie without hesitation in spite of sitting on the porch of the person the sweet confection was intended. If they sat there and ate them all waiting for Kathleen's return, June didn't care because she was having fun she hadn't planned on and Kathleen was just plain missing out.

"You think there's a dipper in the well house?" June said as she got up and made her way around the house to where the well house stood open. A knot of dough swelling in her throat.

"Only one way to find out."

"I'll race you there."

Goldie laughed at the girl's playfulness. She needed to laugh more often. She missed the sound and feel of it.

June smiled over the brim of the white enamel dipper. She licked her lips and hummed a long solid note and the mass washed down with the rush of the cold water. She flipped the dipper in spite of its emptiness but it was the custom and she didn't want Goldie to think she didn't know her manners. June plunged the dipper down into the galvanized bucket resting on the side of the waist high wood bracing supporting the cistern and the rope and watched as the water spilled over the dipper's edges filling it. She passed the dipper to Goldie who drank her fill.

The two stepped out of the cool darkness of the well house and met Kathleen and the baby coming around the corner of the house.

"Hey there! I was beginning to wonder if you left your car and took off on foot." Kathleen said as she met the two in the backyard.

Goldie put her hand out in front of her, the bag of pies not as full as when she left her house with them.

"Made you some fried pies. Peach. You like peach?"

"Yes ma'am peach is just fine but you didn't have to come all the way out here just to bring me these. I was just in town and could have come by your place. As a matter of fact Junebug, I was just at your house."

"My house." June said quickly covering her mouth concealing the smell of peach fried pies and the need to burp.

"Yeah. Won't y'all come inside or let's at least go round to the porch and get out of the sun. I'm wanting to try one of these. I'm sure they are delicious."

Goldie and June followed behind Kathleen and joined her on the front porch after she put the baby in the playpen leaving the front door open so she could keep an eye on her.

Rolling the edges of the paper sack down to the level of the last few pies, Kathleen pulled out three. Goldie and June swallowed deep their stomach brimming with peach fried pies. Politely they thanked Kathleen for sharing and slowly forced down another fried pie.

Chapter Twenty-two

The day was waning and all had grown quiet in Mud Flats. Jimbo slammed the car door hoping to rouse someone from inside the dark house. The sun was setting quickly behind the hill just in front of the house as it made its way through the small hollow crossing one hill, dipping into the valley and climbing up the other side and over the top. He studied his boots while he waited for someone to come to the front door. He had been late getting around to this part of his route today. An endless stack of paperwork piled up from his consistent avoidance of it had reached a point of needing his immediate attention. He knew if he took the sheriff's advice and did the paperwork as it came across his desk instead of avoiding it, it wouldn't become an all day ordeal. Either way he was losing time. Time he'd rather spend on the road and not behind a desk.

Now here he was at his last stop of the day and the report would read just like the others had for the last several months. Status unchanged. He understood the sheriff's directive on following up with Kathleen to make sure she didn't know more about Sonny's disappearance than she let on in the beginning. Now that she was over her baby blues the weekly trip to her place was more bearable. But it was the same story every time. She didn't believe Sonny would desert her and Melody. He was upset over the baby being sick. He was no more equipped to handle that situation than any man would be and she would be the last person to fault him for getting upset. She was always quick to point out that Ellis never minded Sonny borrowing his car and even insisted that Sonny take his car instead of that death trap of a car Sonny was constantly working on. Ellis had a knack for keeping a car running. The two of them could have identical cars and it wouldn't be two weeks before Sonny's was backfiring and burning oil. But, Ellis's would be running fine years later with not a scratch on it. That's how things were from the beginning with the two of them. The

Hatch sisters teased Sonny and Ellis that if they both started the day with a new pair of shoes, Ellis's soles wouldn't have a scuff on them but Sonny's feet would be showing through his. Things always seemed to work out better for Ellis and that was never lost on Sonny but he never said it bothered him. At least, if it did he never let on to anyone, even his wife. Growing up an only child, Sonny never learned the ways of confiding or sharing his thoughts with anyone. Kathleen understood this and accepted it. Ellis did too. His best friend from the cradle, Ellis was always there for Sonny even when Sonny didn't realize it.

Jimbo rapped his knuckles on the door twice more. Called out to the house to see if anyone was going to answer and then turned to walk back to his car. Just as he got across the yard that was more weeds than grass, he heard someone calling out to him from a distance. It was Virginia coming across the pasture on the other side of the road. Jimbo waited for her to reach the yard. She had her apron pulled up in front of her and it was heavy with something.

"Evening." Jimbo called out as Virginia climbed the small embankment from the road. "Getting dark on us. Sun will be gone directly." Eyeing her turned up apron full of blackberries he stated the obvious struggling to make polite conversation, "You been picking blackberries?"

"Yeah." Virginia said out of breath from coming across the pasture and through the barbed wire fencing faster than she normally would. Seeing Jimbo waiting in front of Kathleen and Sonny's she wanted to get to him before he left. She didn't like that he made these weekly visits. In her opinion they did more harm than good. If Sonny was gone he was gone. And, that should be enough to settle it for everyone. But not enough for the sheriff or Jimbo or both. She wasn't sure which it was. Considering how things went the last two times she saw Jimbo and the dark mood she was in today, she had nothing to lose by finding out.

Pouring out the contents of her apron into an enamel washbowl on Kathleen's front porch, Virginia said, "Yeah. I came across the bushes sometime last year. Didn't get anything off of them then. The cows got to them before I did or maybe it was Ellis's sisters. Thought if I was going to get any this year I better beat the heifers." She laughed at her own joke and didn't wait for Jimbo to find the humor in it.

"Guess you're wondering where Kathleen is?" Virginia said. She made no attempt to hide her snickering expression.

"Looks like no one's home." Jimbo said. He tried looking into the dark windows without being too obvious. The last thing he needed at the end of a trying day was to lock horns with Virginia Hatch.

"Looks that way." Virginia goaded.

"Any idea when she'll be back."

"Didn't know she was gone. Guess that's the way things go around here. Folks just come and go as they please." Virginia said. He words sharp as darts.

"You saying she's gone for good?"

"Ain't saying nothing like that. Just saying she's gone. That's all. We mind our own business around here. Not sure how you folks do it in town." Virginia said. Her back bowed up readying for a fight.

Jimbo rubbed the blonde stubble on his chin. A nervous tick he tried to control. "Virginia, I don't mean no disrespect. I'm just trying to do my job."

"And you're job is coming around here once a week to do what exactly?

"You know what. The sheriff doesn't need to explain official police business."

Virginia laughed at how quickly Jimbo got riled up. He didn't like doing it. That was obvious to her as the nose on his face.

"Jimbo, if you don't like coming out here. Why do it. Nothing is any different today than it was the first day you came out here back in the winter. Looks to me if anything you are causing more harm than good. At least to yourself not mention the rest of us."

Jimbo guarded his reaction. He wasn't sure what Virginia thought she knew but she apparently was trying to make a point. He had played enough poker in his life to know what a person looks like when they think they are holding all the cards. Virginia had the look of a royal flush.

Thinking through his next move Jimbo was reminded of one of the many lectures his father gave him and his brothers about dealing with people. Morgan Bishop believed and led his boys to believe people were all alike in desperate times. He told his boys it was his experience that generation after generation was convinced that creation was controlled by a cosmic cause and effect. He'd say religions were built on it. Lives were shaped by it. You push. I pull. And if it is God's will, we'll meet in the middle. Morgan lectured his boys that whether a person attended church every Sunday or was moved by emotions at a tent revival, what passed for faith in God was usually nothing more than superstition. The elder Bishop wanted his sons to know the difference between what looked godly and what was.

Jimbo had seen it all his life. Like a second skin, people wore their religion to remind everyone including God who they were in this world. Virginia Hatch wore hers with pride believing it somehow separated her from the rest making her superior than most. She had something to say and Jimbo knew if he gave her time and space to say it, he'd find out just what was going on in this hollow of secrets and shadows.

"What kinda harm you talking about Virginia? I don't see how me doing my job is harming anyone." Jimbo sat down on the edge of the porch giving the pretense of contrition leaving Virginia to stand over him giving her the sense of having the upper hand. He had seen Sheriff Bright do it when he was trying to get a confession out of someone. Make them believe you need their insight and they'll tell you more than you'd ever get from asking straightforward questions. People want to talk, he'd say time and time again, you just got to give them the space and time to do it. The sheriff was right. Virginia was in need of confession.

Separated by a wall of darkness. The sun long gone from the hollow and the moon hidden behind the house. Virginia sat down on a ladder back chair, holding to her position of power, and spoke as if sitting in the confessional booth.

"I don't know what others have been telling you but I'm telling you I had nothing to do with Sonny Price taking off like he did. People walk around their whole lives holding to secrets that eventually get told. I can't be held responsible for someone else's secrets. Everything will come out in the end. That's just the way it is. Least ways that's what I believe. No sense trying to live like it ain't the truth. It's the truth whether you believe it or not. Don't change things just because you don't believe. Like I said, I don't know what's been said to you or who's been doing the talking. No sense fretting over who said what and why." Virginia paused, shifted her weight in the ladder back chair, cleared her throat and fought against a wall of emotion. "If I knew things was going to end like they did that morning. If I knew Sonny was going to fly off the handle like he did. If I could go back and change things I would. Believe me. I would. Just because you can unwind the hands of the clock don't mean you can turn back time. I've wrestled with this for months now and I'm telling you, I believe Sonny should have known the truth long before I said anything to him. I can't be held accountable for other people's actions. If he's dead. I can't be held responsible." She paused again to rein in her emotions and tap into her courage. "I just believe there's no way he couldn't have known all these years how every one of them involved tried to protect him and his mama and now here at the end, it may have just cost him his life. That's if you believe he's dead. But I don't. I don't because I've seen him since." Another small pause to catch her breath and shift her weight in the chair and her chin a little higher in defense. "Saw him cut across that tobacco field just like he did the morning the baby got sick. Saw it as plain as day. I couldn't sleep. Up with one of my headaches, sometimes all I can do is walk the floors and wait for relief and that's when I saw him. From back just beyond the back field, back towards Ellis's mama and daddy's place, across the field and towards the house there. He walked all the way around it. Stopped for a spell, I thought at the time he was coming home, trying to enter the house quiet like as not to frighten Kathleen or wake the baby, but just as the idea was taking shape in my sore and pounding head, he was gone. As fast as he appeared he was gone and I ain't seen him since. Of course there's been plenty others that have come by, you for one and Arvis Ange the other. Can't say I knew Arvis Ange had any business in Mud Flats till Sonny went missing. There's something to that but I'm not saying what 'cause I've already said too much. And, I can't say anything to Kathleen about it. It just wouldn't be my place to bring it up to her. I know it's probably been said I had something to do with Sonny racing out into that ice storm and off the ridge, and that I should apologize or something to Kathleen for it. But I know if I brought it up to her I'd be just piling misery on top of misery. And, I just ain't got the stomach for it. I don't care what anyone says. Everyone thinks I'm the strong one. I ain't no stronger than the next one. My name may be Hatch but I know better than to go wagging my tongue around town telling everyone my business. If minding your own business makes you stronger than the next person than maybe I am stronger than the rest of them."

Jimbo would have sat in the darkness all night if it meant Virginia would keep talking but her confession had played out and his self-control was nearly gone. She had said all her conscious and pride would allow. He understood and knew if she was willing to unburden herself once she would be seeking opportunities to rid herself again of whatever was eating away at her insides. Like Ruskin said, give them time and people will tell you everything you need to know. Jimbo was willing to give Virginia all the time she needed.

They sat in silence for a while letting the atmosphere around them settle back down to the peaceful ease of the falling evening until a car rumbled by severing the quiet moment. Virginia made excuses about needing to get to her house and get the blackberries on the stove and Jimbo took his leave knowing he only had to wait a week.

Chapter Twenty-three

A small mountain of headless chickens lay bleeding out beside a cast iron drum of icy salt water. One by one Sonny plucked the birds clean of their feathery covering and dropped them into the kettle. They sank to the bottom only to rise to the top and dance under the blocks of ice. His hands matted with dried blood and feathers moved as if they belonged to someone else, while his mind wondered to places unseen. He was lost in a loneliness that haunted him, like a cold advancing wind that crawled up his bones and snaked its way to his heart, making him heart sick for something unknown but familiar, something lost that he never knew he had.

He watched his hands pull the feathers from the prickly skin and remembered someone else's hands doing the same thing. He remembered with the eyes of a child. His hands remembered too. That's how they knew what to do working without any thoughtful direction from him. He let his eyes roam up his arms leaving his hands to do their job hoping this time he would see the face that belonged to the hands he saw in his mind. Like trying to see past the white edges of a photograph, to see the unseen story, he cannot see past the point of the still shots of his memories to know who he is remembering. Hands that look like his. Strong and firm but loving and gentle. Hands that know how to do things. Things he too knows how to do. The memories are trapped deep inside of him, down in the place where secrets are kept.

"You bout got them chickens ready?" Arvis bellowed from the kitchen screen door.

"Just about." Sonny plucked quicker pulling his thoughts back front and center. He owed Arvis Ange a lot but he wasn't about to pay him with his soul.

"You look like your daddy sitting there working them chickens."

Sonny's heart clutched in his chest like someone had reached in and grabbed it. He couldn't feel himself breathing and it felt like time had sudden stopped moving. A roar like a thousand voices saying the same thing flooded his ears. He could see Arvis's mouth moving as he came near him but he couldn't hear anything but the rush of voices.

"You hear me boy? You okay? That blood ain't making you sick is it? The feathers don't smell too pretty after a while either do they? Nope, a body has to have a gift for certain things in life. And your daddy was one of them. I've seen him do things other men only brag about. You understand the difference between doing and bragging? Your daddy wasn't a braggart that's for dang sure but if anybody had a reason for bragging it'd been him."

He bit a plug off the twist of tobacco he kept in the bid pocket of his overalls and between long hard chews and a few cursory spits, Arvis kept reminiscing not noticing the affect his recollections were having on Sonny. Laughing as he remembered he said. "It was me and your daddy and a cousin of your mama's. Course she wasn't your mama at the time. No, we were just tadpoles at the time. But we thought we were grown." He laughed censoring his thoughts. "We thought we were sharp but we were dull as a froe." Laughing again in spite of himself, "And didn't have the good sense to know the difference." He paused waiting for the memory to form into words. "I don't recollect just which one of us thought of it first and if you'd asked us we'd all take credit for it but now that I think back on it I reckon it was your daddy was the one that convinced us. That's just how your daddy was. He was a smooth talker. That's for sure and there's no denying it." His words clipped with laughter. "You're living proof of that."

Sonny's spine went straight like a ramrod and the chicken he had been plucking fell between his feet. He hadn't heard anyone speak so freely about his parents, especially his father, since he was a small boy. Arvis noticed the reaction but didn't say anything too drunk on reliving the memory spinning in his head to worry about how it all must sound to Sonny.

"It must have been the last night of the full moon. We'd done all the mischief three young'uns could get into when your daddy decided he had a taste for fried chicken. Baxter Burns prided himself on the best eggs and poultry on the ridge and it didn't take your daddy too long to make his mind up to help himself to a couple of old man Burns's prized hens. Well what we didn't know but soon found out the hard way was old man Burns had had a run of bad luck that week with something from the woods getting in his chicken coop and helping itself to a chicken dinner. Guess your daddy wasn't the first one to have that idea. That particular night old man Burns had been waiting in the shadows for whatever it was to make its way out of the dark and into the clearing." Arvis chucked as he released a dark brown stream of tobacco juice from over his stained thick bottom lip. Sonny was captivated by the story listening like a child sitting on the edge of his seat. His flesh rippling with goose bumps and chills.

"Well I don't know who was more surprised us or old man Burns. Just about the time we rounded the corner of that chicken coop with a chicken under each arm, he lit us up with buck shot sending us running for cover and feathers flying." Arvis choked on his laughter and chaw of tobacco and almost lost his balance reared back too far on his heels.

Caught up in the story, Sonny reached down and picked up the half-naked chicken laying between his feet and started plucking again anticipating the ending to the story.

"Son, I've got to tell you, by the time we stopped running and settled down, that was the best tasting chicken I've ever ate, buckshot and all!"

They both laughed as the images of the story settle in around them like invisible visitors. Sonny continued plucking and dropping the bare birds into the icy water. Arvis stood. Stretched his bowed legs and then squatted again taking advantage of the opportunity to test the waters of time with Sonny.

"How old are you boy? You seen your twenty-first birthday yet?

"Last year. Matter of fact, my birthday was two weeks ago."

"Son. Son. This ain't no way to be celebrating a milestone such as that. You here when your family is over there. I wouldn't be surprised if they ain't still wondering all this time where you are. How you're getting on."

"Been gone too long to go back now. Anyways, you've seen Kathleen. The way you tell it she's doing just fine without me. I'm just a ghost to her now."

"That ain't the way I see it and I know it ain't the way your mama and daddy would have seen it. Your daddy for certain. How old were you when he let out?"

"I don't know. Three. Maybe four. Too young to remember."

"No. No. You got part of it right. You don't remember. I was there. And you were older than three or four. If I was guessing it was more like six. You and Ram's boy ain't but a few months apart in age. I remember Milly going on at the time about you boys starting school that fall and how your mama was going to need help."

"I don't know nothing about all of that."

Sonny dropped the last chicken in the water and felt his shoulders drop too ready to take on the weight of whatever Arvis was about to unload on him. A crow called out from the cover of a nearby tree giving credibility to Arvis playing witness to Sonny's fractured past.

"Take it from someone who was there. Yours and Ellis's mama were as round as the moon and Ram and Tinkum were puffed up and scratching the ground around them like a couple Banty roosters. Don't get me wrong, Son, I ain't one to judge. I've known your people from way back. And your mama was as good as gold but she loved your daddy just like your aunt did and it was your daddy who in the end had to make the choice. I can't fault him for it. At the time, it all seemed to be happening so fast. And, well, we thought we knew more about things than we did just like you young'uns think you know so much. Looking back, sure there were things that could have been done differently, but you can't go back and change what was."

Sonny swallowed the knot of emotion hard as walnut lodged in his throat. Everything Virginia had said to him in the emergency room was true. She might have been angry for her own reasons. And, it wasn't her truth to tell but hers or not, it was out there. It had been boring like a bee in his brain for months and now hearing it from someone who gained nothing by sharing it, someone who was there and saw it firsthand, the bee bore through the last remaining layer of what separated him from the truth. He knew now. It was his truth. And he couldn't run from it any longer.

"Well, like I said. That's the way I see is all. And, like I said before. Spending your birthday here with the likes of me instead of over there with your woman and baby just ain't right no matter how you try to slice it. I've said it before and I'll say it again, you're welcome to stay here as long as you want. It's the least I can do but I'm telling you now and then I'll keep my peace, whatever it is you're running from ain't going to stop chasing you until you stop running. It's just that simple."

Arvis stood and patted his pocket for his truck keys. Reached in for them and said he was going over the state line to see a man about some timber. Said he'd leave Sonny to finish plucking the chickens and then wrap them and put them in the deep freeze in the well house. Said he had plans to sell them to the grocery store in town and didn't need them to ruin before he made it to town. Sonny nodded and turned his attention to removing the chickens from the icy water leaving Arvis to drive off without another word.

* * *

The moon hung low in the evening sky and Sonny watched as Kathleen bent over putting her head through the car window. He could hear women's voices and laughter and wondered if it was Kathleen that made the joke or was she laughing at someone else's humor. He missed the sound of her laughter and it made him laugh under his breath. Sitting in the tall grass like an animal of prey, he waited for the Buick to roll out of sight and for Kathleen to make her way into the dark house using the passing car's headlights to light the way.

Between the blades of tall grass, he watched as one by

one the windows spilled yellow light onto the dirt patches below their sashes. He knew her routine like the back of his hand. She would give the baby a sponge bath in the wash pan she used for the dishes. He held his breath removing all other sound hoping to hear her singing to the baby. But between the chirping crickets and the distance, he couldn't hear her.

His eyes strained to see her pass in front of the window as she put the baby down for the night and then curl up on their bed to read one of her mail order romance novels. His heart pulled at him as he remembered how he use to tease her about cutting out brown paper sacks for book covers to hide what she was reading. She took it well and he hoped now that she wasn't hiding a private hurt in her heart by something stupid he had said. Trying to be funny and clever to impress her seemed harmless at the time. Now it felt like a huge wedge separating him even more from her. A wedge he created.

He wanted to go to her. Say he was sorry for running out on her and the baby. He wanted to rest his head once more in her lap and empty his heart to her. But this time, empty it completely. He wanted to tell her what Virginia had said. How she was folded into the family secret on her wedding night. How she was sworn to oblige the family by never sharing their truth to anyone. To carry it to her grave. He wanted to tell her how his heart hurt like an old forgotten wound ripped open fresh when he heard what Virginia said to him in the emergency room. How it scared him. How defeated he already felt and how insignificant her words made him feel. He wanted her to know he survived the crash. That the thing he had bragged about for ages was something he was actually capable of doing. Rolling from the moving car. Freeing himself from the impending crash. He wanted her to know it was not intentional. He believed like he was taught. That the deer must have been the hand of God. He didn't doubt it. He didn't question it. He just kept running. He wanted to tell her it was him that had Arvis Ange checking on her. Trading with her. That his guns and tools were all safe with him and that Arvis had no need for them and that it was his hard work on Arvis's place that bought her the meat, produce and fresh milk from Arvis. He also wanted her to know that Arvis did him one better and gave him back his memories of his daddy. That everything Virginia said was out of pain. But what Arvis shared was out of love. He knew what it was like to make hard choices in life. And that he was still learning. He wanted her to know he chose her.

But with all the well-wishing he was making he was still sitting hunkered down in the cover of the tall sweet grass under the glow of the full moon and Kathleen might as well be on the other side of the moon because for now he was as good as a ghost to her and everyone else.

Chapter Twenty-four

June sat in the back booth at Patti Cake's Diner wrapping a folded paper napkin around her finger and missing her home. She wrapped and unwrapped the napkin as her mind wrapped and unwrapped the plans she had made for her wedding. It had been three days since she announced at the supper table that she wasn't going to marry Jimbo. Seen and not heard had been the rule all her life at the table. It was the rule for her whole life. She had come to accept it without question. Why she chose to say anything was still a mystery to her. Her parents so lost in their own lives never paid any particular interest in hers or at least that's the way it appeared to her. So when her daddy asked her to pass the cornbread, she not only passed him the plate she served it up with her announcement that she was not going to marry Jimbo. Her daddy didn't flinch. That night she had her bags packed, and no explanation other than she was going to stay at Mrs. Filbry's for the summer, June left her parent's house after the supper dishes were washed and put away leaving her parents to put two and two together on their own.

Patti Cake's Diner filled quickly with young couples grabbing a bite to eat before going to the drive-in and with older couples out for their payday night-on-the-town before going to the grocery store for a week's worth of groceries.

June slurped the last bit of her chocolate milkshake up through the straw scrapping the bottom of the glass to taste the last of the chocolate syrup trapped at the bottom. The sound of an engine coughing like a two-pack-a-day smoker followed by the solid slam of the car's heavy door meant Mrs. Filbry had just pulled into the parking lot. Within seconds the crowded diner was filled with an electric current that seemed to vibrate off of Goldalena Filbry wherever she went. Her voice was recognizable over the hum of private conversations as she made her way around the room saying hello and shaking hands with this one than that one like a seasoned politician. June felt her face curl up into a smile watching her elderly friend work the room. It looked natural and she admired and envied Mrs. Filbry's grace and ease. She wanted to be like that and wondered if Mrs. Filbry had always been so outgoing and familiar with everyone she met or if it was something she acquired over her lifetime. The paper napkin slid off of June's finger leaving a pink indention where the blood was beginning to flow back from her fingertip. She was more relaxed now that Mrs. Filbry was here. Adjusting her body in the booth, she smiled and waited for her turn for a dose of Goldie Filbry.

Patti met Goldie at the table, turned the coffee cup over onto its saucer and filled it. "I'll be right back with your cream." Patti said turning to retrieve the cream for Goldie's coffee. June could see that it pleased Mrs. Filbry to be so familiar with the diner's owner that she knew just how she liked her coffee but she detected a slight irritation too that the cream was not ready and waiting. Or maybe that was June's imagination because Mrs. Filbry never acted as though she expected any exceptional treatment. It just came to her. Maybe that was her own expectation she was feeling.

Looking around at the tables she just passed Goldie said, "By the looks of this place, don't reckon anyone cooks at home anymore." June winced at the comment thinking about her parents and the suffocating silence she left at their supper table. Her parents would never consider going out to eat no matter the occasion. She was glad Goldie didn't see her reaction. She didn't want to invite suspicion where there was no need for it.

"Patti Ann, you're doing a lot of business for a week night." Goldie said as Patti poured cream into the untouched cup of coffee. Standing upright to stretch the tired muscles in her lower back, Patti smiled.

"Not bad for a Friday night. Guess folks see it as the beginnings to their weekend."

"Humph, weekend. Just one more day on the calendar as far as I can tell."

"Goldie Filbry, where do you get all your sunshine?"

"Same place you get yours dearie."

Patti and Goldie laughed at the private joke forgetting about the young and naïve girl sitting ringside for their unusual conversation. She knew it had more meaning than what they were letting on and tucked it away in the recesses of her mind to chew on later. Her eyes followed Patti around the room as she retraced the steps that Goldie had just taken. Stopping at every table and spending just enough time at each to spread her own brand of sunshine. Part of June was beginning to put it together but she hadn't learned to trust that part of herself.

"Well, I'm going to sit here and enjoy this cup of coffee. You want anything?" Goldie asked not paying any particular interest in the empty milkshake glass sitting between her and June.

"No ma'am. I just finished off this milkshake before you got here." June shifted her weight to the right sitting a little closer to her blue and green tapestry overnight bag embarrassed that she had it with her debating on whether to stay with Mrs. Filbry or go back home. It had been the official bag from Avon when her aunt Della had decided one summer to become an Avon lady. Going door-to-door selling lotions and lipsticks to women that rarely wore powder soon became a fool's errand for Della. Discouraged she no longer wanted to have the cosmetics around her as a reminder of her failure so she didn't put up any resistance when June, too young for makeup at the time, asked for them. Not only did she get the bags of samples meant to be given to customers to encourage future sales but she got the pretty tapestry suitcase too. That whole summer June tried on the various foundations and lipsticks trying to find one she could wear outside the safety and privacy of her bedroom without being asked what was on her face and being made to watch it off immediately. The embarrassment was enough to not want to every wear makeup and she wondered many times after her one and only scourging from her daddy if that was why most women she knew didn't wear any.

That was another reason why she enjoyed Goldie Filbry and Florence Bright's company. Although they both grew up in and around Scots Ridge just like everyone else she knew, they were so much different that everyone else. Goldie and Florence both wore makeup every day. Just a little powder and lipstick on most days and on occasion a little mascara. It made June feel pretty just being near them and she too wanted to know how to wear a little powder and lipstick and be just as pretty as they made her feel.

Spying the small suitcase Goldie asked, "Did your mama and daddy say something about you coming to stay with me? Do I need to give them a call or go by and see them?" Goldie watched June over the rim of her coffee cup. She knew the answer because she knew June's mama and daddy. She knew Ella wouldn't speak her mind if her life depended on it. She was ready to lose her daughter to a boy that wouldn't treat her any different than she had been treated by the hateful boy that grew into the hateful man she married. She didn't know any better for herself and didn't know how to know any better for her only daughter. Goldie wanted to feel sorry for Ella but she had long since quit feeling sorry for people too lazy to see life march right in front of them and not willing to step in time with it.

Goldie knew all too well the brand of hatefulness that swelled in Cotton's belly. He had worked every day of his life from the time he was old enough to carry a milk bucket to drag a hoe in the garden. All he knew was work so it made sense that he would forget how to laugh and appreciate the gifts God had given him in the love and care of a good woman and the adoration a daughter can bring. Goldie came all too close to Cotton's sour disposition when she was courting her husband and if it hadn't been for her Henry stepping in and claiming what he believed was his, Goldie could be sitting across the table at Patti Cake's Diner with her daughter instead of Ella's. But, that was history long forgotten and she didn't have the energy or interest in stirring it up. She was more than happy to do anything June wanted tind taking her home or giving her a place to stay while she worked things out in her heart and mind, then that was the least she could do. As best as Goldie could tell, the young people in Tillman had a lot more to deal with in this day and time than she and those her age did back when they were young.

"No ma'am, no need to call or visit them. I'm fine. I

mean, they're fine. They understand." June said through a half-hearted smile and spun the straw in the empty glass. She stopped just as she saw Goldie watching her and hoped she wasn't misunderstood. She didn't want another milkshake and she didn't want to bother her parents. What she wanted was to forget all she knew and learn. Learn from this woman that had so much to teach.

"Well, I'll take your word for it. I see you've got your suitcase there. Do you need anything? I don't reckon Ben Franklin's is still open at this hour." Goldie knew that sounded stupid. Of course Ben Franklin's wasn't open this late in the evening. None of the stores were open on the Square at this hour. "But, we could drive over to the A&P, if you think you need anything. Or we can get out tomorrow and pick up a few things."

June was embarrassed for not knowing how to answer. Everything she owned was in the suitcase beside her. What more could she need? Surely there was something she was forgetting or supposed to be needing but was too ignorant or misguided to know to need it or ask for it. Mrs. Filbry looked and sounded a bit nervous. Surely she had all the answers and wasn't uncertain about this new arrangement or the reason June was sitting there with her clothes packed. June refused to consider that as a possibility and decided on believing instead that whatever this mysterious need was that she would discover it soon enough. Besides, the stores were closed except for the A&P and as far as she knew, there was nothing there but groceries.

"No ma'am can't think of anything I need. Least ways not tonight. If it comes to me, I can always walk up to the Square from your house and pick it up." June smiled but the smile fell fast as she saw out of the corner of her eye the uniform. She always saw the uniform before she saw the young lean body that filled it. Jimbo had walked in to the diner and was making his way across the room to the counter.

"We can leave now if you want to. You don't have to stay here. You just tell me what you want." Goldie's voice sounded more like June's conscience speaking to her. Lost in the thought of him and all the promises that were made, June tried hard to decide what to do. She had been pulled by an invisible string tied to Jimbo for so long that she didn't know how to tread this new ground untethered.

"Speak now or forever hold your..." Goldie was once again speaking but June wasn't sure if she was hearing what the woman was saying or hearing her own thoughts. As if by her thoughts she caused him to turn around, Jimbo leaned onto the counter with the familiar ease that stirred something deep inside June. She knew she was holding her breath but was afraid if she exhaled she would wake up and realize it was all a dream. Dreaming or not, he was there and was looking in her direction. Looking but not seeing. It was when she felt the hot tear roll down her cheek and felt the heat from Mrs. Filbry's palm on the back of her hand that she knew she had been this close to him and he didn't see her. Cold waves of realization washed over her from head to toe and in a moment that felt like a lifetime she finally saw what everyone had seen. Wisdom gave her a small glimpse and she knew she would forever be grateful.

With one hand she dried the moist trail left by the tear and with the other she grasped Mrs. Filbry's hand and said she was ready to leave. Without hesitation, Goldie got up from her seat in the booth and made her way out the diner's door not stopping to speak to anyone but quietly and with much determination made her way to her car with June a few paces behind her. Nearing her car she fished her keys out of her pants pocket and reaches to open the door.

"Hey y'all wait up. June you going to just leave and not speak. That's not like you." Jimbo said walking across the parking lot. His words land like rocks hurled in spite just missing their intended target. Goldie waits for June in the car and makes no attempt to avoid hearing the conversation. She can clearly make out what Jimbo is saying. Anyone within a car's length can hear what Jimbo is saying as he makes no effort to keep his voice down. But, only he can hear June's response to his disguised concern.

"Junie what's going on with you? It's not like you to

walk right by and not speak." Jimbo reaches out to take her by the hand but she doesn't respond to his false humility keeping her hand free from his touch.

"Wrong? Nothing with me. We were on our way out. Sorry if I didn't see you."

"We. Who's we?" Jimbo says looking around the parking lot.

"Mrs. Filbry and me. I'm staying over at her house for the summer."

"And, why are you doing such a fool thing as that? What'd your mama and daddy say about that?" Jimbo says. His feet planted and his arms crossed making his point and asserting his authority.

"As a matter of fact they didn't say anything. I guess they figure if I'm old enough to get married. I'm old enough to make decisions on my own about where I want to spend my summer."

June saw the effect her mentioning marriage had on Jimbo and knew it was hurting him as much as it was hurting her to be this near and not be touching. She had decided just in the last few minutes of the evening that Jimbo couldn't have it both ways. Seeing him now and feeling this surge of surety race through her veins reinforced her.

"I can't see why anyone in their right mind would want to spend a summer, a whole summer, cooped up at some old widow woman's house. June the things you do will forever confound me." Jimbo said. He started to laugh but then thought better of it.

"Well, thank goodness for you James Conroy Bishop, I'm not your concern."

"So it's like that is it? We postpone the wedding and you decide you're going to be your own woman. Just go about as if we never were a couple. Never had any plans. Is that how it is?"

Again, June saw the hurt swimming under his skin.

"I can't say."

"What do you mean you can't say? What's gotten into you woman? You're not acting like yourself."

"Maybe I am. Maybe this is me. This is the me you never paid any attention to. Maybe this is the me you should have paid attention to. Because maybe, just maybe, had you paid attention to me long enough to see me, really see me, you'd know exactly what I'm doing and wouldn't be standing here in this parking lot making a fool out of both of us."

June had no idea what any of that meant and she had no idea where it came from. It was as if someone else had taken possession of her body and was speaking through her. The words sounded as confusing to her as they did to Jimbo by the stunned look on his face. And just as she measured the emotion rising between them, it fell into a dark and vengeful place that she knew all too well from when she had sassed her daddy. The look on Jimbo's face told the tale.

"Fool. There's only one fool standing here. And that's you."

June forced her feet to move in spite of the feeling like she had been glued to the parking lot asphalt. Jimbo glared at her waiting for her response. She didn't offer one other than to turn around and get into Mrs. Filbry's idling car.

The brake lights glowed red on his pants legs as he stood his ground in the diner's parking lot watching old lady Filbry and the woman he loves drive away

Chapter Twenty-five

Goldie drove around the Square and out the highway letting the cool evening air fill the car through open windows and mix with the low volume of the radio as it spilled out one song after another from the country music station in Nashville. The night was clear and the radio station was coming in clear as a bell with no sizzling static. There was no hurry in getting home and she knew June needed time to wrestle her thoughts and emotions into submission. She didn't hear what June had to say to Jimbo. She could only hear what Jimbo was saying and like everyone else within earshot of the two in the parking lot, she didn't make any effort in avoiding to eavesdrop. His deputy sheriff uniform demanded attention but it was obvious to a blind man that their conversation was personal. Anyone that knew the two knew that just like most kids that grew up in these parts once they began showing interest in one another they were bound to get married when their age or body determined it. Whichever came first?

By anyone's estimation their quarrel wasn't any different than any other quarrel between two unmarried people. It was sport to those seasoned in matrimony and still speaking, and a bruise to the tender mercies once felt by those that were married but no longer spoke to one another, other than what was absolutely necessary to manage the day.

Like Goldie and her late husband, Jimbo's parents were like the former. Still enjoying the lively banter between two people that not only loved each other but also enjoyed one another's company more than their own. Unlike the later and June's parents that became stifled and silent soon after the ceremony and would rather sit alone than to share a moment in the company of the other.

Goldie listened as Eddie Arnold's smooth voice poured from the car speaker as he sang about love. She wondered how anyone could live like June's parents and before Eddie hit his last note she was once again missing her husband.

"Mama listens to this station." June rested her head on the car seat and looked out the window at the tree line grow darker and darker along the highway. Goldie drove on quietly letting her speak and relieve her mind from its worries.

"We've got a radio on top of the refrigerator and she keeps it turned to WSM. I don't think it has ever been changed." June laughs then corrects herself. "Well, except for that one time I changed it to a station to hear Elvis Presley." She laughs again remembering. "But that didn't last long. Daddy came flying through the door and with the same hand whooped me good and changed the station back to where it had been." She laughs again at the memory and the empty spot where the pain once lived. "Yeah, I didn't bother the radio anymore after that. Elvis or no Elvis. The radio was off limits."

June sat quietly for a couple of minutes. Eased down in the seat adjusting to the relaxation filling her body. And, Goldie kept driving around the outskirts of town avoiding any possible intrusions with a certain curious deputy sheriff.

"Funny how you remember things. I don't think I even knew daddy listened to the radio. And, there he was lickety-split ready to tan my hid for changing the station. I don't even know where came from. He was moving so fast. One minute he wasn't there, the next minute he was and then poof gone again. Oh well, that was then and this is now. Guess I don't have to worry about any man getting hot under the collar about anything I say or do anymore. As of tonight, I'm no longer under my daddy's roof and well, I guess I don't have to worry about any other man's roof either."

Suddenly, June felt her comments may have sounded disrespectful to Mrs. Filbry and she sat up quickly and began to apologize. But, Goldie assured her she had nothing to worry about. She understood exactly what she meant and there was no harm done. June eased back into her relaxed state and accepted Mrs. Filbry's answer without any objection. It was the first time she ever resisted doubt and wondered if it no longer had a hold on her.

Two more times around town and once more out the

highway and back was enough to give June time to let go of her resistance to change. Goldie knew it was a struggle to let go. She had spent enough of her own life letting go to know what it looked like. Pulling the car into the driveway she noticed the lights were on at Florence's house and the patrol car was not in the driveway. She'd get June settled inside then walk over and check on Florence. It was too late for Ruskin to still be at work and she knew from the number of lights left on they were not out together.

The hairs on the back of Goldie's neck stood on end as she thought of Florence sitting home alone another night this week. Thinking back she calculated Ruskin had been gone a total of six nights in a row with tonight being seven if he was indeed gone on official business.

"June let's get you set up in here. You can put your things in this dresser and I've cleared out the closet for you too if you have need of it. There's clean sheets on the bed and an extra blanket in the cedar chest if you think you'll need one. Help yourself to the bathroom and if you need anything I'll be right back. I'm going to walk over and check on Florence."

Goldie felt a smile pull at the corners of her mouth and her shoulders to drop ever so slightly as she walked back through her house and out the front door. She glanced toward her husband's chair as was her habit and sent him a loving thought. This one was about June and how happy she was to have someone in the house with her again.

June made herself at home putting her clothes away in the dresser drawers. She loved the smell of the lavender tissue paper that lined each drawer and opened and closed the drawers between each trip from the suitcase to the dresser just to soak in the light cheerful fragrance. She wanted it for hers. If she could feel the way the lavender smelled she thought she could be happy all the time. Leaving a little trail of happiness in her wake as she passed by, then everyone would know she was content in her new life and never doubt her or her decision.

The bathroom was tidy and everything in its rightful place. This would be something she would soon add to her catalog of new traits. Organization had to be as important as cleanliness and if so, could only be as virtuous.

The heat of the shower coupled with the glycerin soap she found in the soap dish soothed her mind and body. She showered until the water ran cool and then stood in the tub with the shower curtain pulled back, something she would never had dared to do at home. She didn't actually remember being taught any of her parents' rules. They were just there like the kudzu that grew along the roadside. Taking over and straggling everything in its path. But, tonight as she stood in the tub, the steam rising off her bare body, she looked around the bathroom with no fear of any kind.

Hanging the wet towels on the metal towel rack on the back of the bathroom door, June turned to gather up her clothes from the floor and the half empty bottle of lotion from the last of the Avon samples, when she heard the sound of a door slam from behind the house. Knowing better than to call out to Mrs. Filbry, just one more of her daddy's rules she learned from an early age to never call out if you hear something but instead slowly make your way to where you'd expect your help to come, in this case it would be Mrs. Filbry but the last she knew, Mrs. Filbry was across the street.

June tossed her things onto the bed in the guest room all the while listening to hear if anyone was in the house or outside behind the house. She tip toed down the hall and noticed the front door standing open. She peeked around the corner of the hall just enough to look out the front door and across the street to Florence's house. She could see Florence and Goldie talking on the front porch. The light from inside the house illuminating their silhouettes well enough that June could see each gesture and read their body language. She could tell when Florence was talking. As her hands moved in front of her chest slow and steady like when you are trying to protect yourself and your position. She could also tell when Goldie was speaking because her hands were splayed open like big funeral home fans on the ends of her arms going up and down as if she was trying to capture a big wind and take flight. June could stand there all night watching the animated conversation and imagine what they could be discussing but the sound of the cellar door slamming again made her leave the floor in a startled jump. She stood frozen fearing what was outside. Her eyes never left the conversation across the street and she could tell they too heard the door slam. Within seconds, the two dark shadows were now cutting across Mrs. Filbry's front yard and June could hear their voices as clearly as if they were standing in the hall with her.

"Wait Goldie, you're going to fall running in the dark!" Florence said. She was two strides behind.

"If I get my hands on that hooligan you'll have more to worry about than my banged up knees!"

June ran out the front door and after Florence and Goldie. By the time she made it to the back yard, she once again saw them standing in the light that fell from the house like a spot light, near the cellar door.

"What...who...?" June had only ran a few paces but was completely out of breath compared to her two elders who stood looking around, their hands on their hips, and their lungs fully recovered from their sprint across the street.

"I don't know. But we heard it. Did you?" Florence asked assuming June had to have heard the cellar door slam just as they did from across the street.

"She don't know. I've not had time to tell her about it." Goldie said as she panned the back yard and the tree line that skirted her property separating her from the overgrown woods. Florence looked at Goldie and then back at June. June didn't sense that Florence was as concerned about her knowing the mystery of the slamming door as she as about Goldie taking matters into her own hands.

"I've told her she needs to let me say something to Ruskin..." Florence started to explain just as Goldie's hand stopped her from speaking any further.

"Florence, I told you I know who it is and it is my intention to catch him and deal with him my own way."

June suddenly became intrigued as her curiosity replaced her fear.

"What in the world? You know who? What?" June asked almost laughing at the strangeness of the situation.

"She thinks she knows who is sneaking into her cellar and stealing from her and she plans to catch him and teach him a lesson. Without, might I add, troubling the law? Who just so happens to live right across the street and is more than willing and happy to oblige her at any hour of the day." Florence said.

June giggled nervously. She couldn't help herself, but Florence or Goldie didn't seem to notice or mind. Here these two women she admired were cackling like a couple of old hens while an intruder was nearby.

"I'm fully aware of who lives across the street and I know just like you know, my dear, just how busy he is. And, I think we all know if we catch one we'll catch the other."

June gasped at the same time Florence gasped. Florence, like June, was curious who besides Sonny Price was missing.

Chapter Twenty-six

June pulls the pan back and forth across the eye on the stove waiting for the butter to heat the popcorn kernels sending them smacking against the pan lid. The glow of the TV fluttered like bats escaping the darkness of a cave as the first scene of the creature feature spread across the screen. Curled up on the couch she settled in with her bowl of popcorn and a bottle of Dr. Pepper. Goldie said help yourself and June was obliging. Helping herself to the kitchen and the freedom to stay up and watch the late show until the signal ended and the screen was filled with snow and static.

The bathroom door opened and closed and Goldie walked down the dark hallway and crossed in front of June and sat beside her on the couch. Reaching in for a handful of popcorn she mentioned that her husband enjoyed staying up for the late show and enjoyed the creature feature. June liked the familiarity Goldie was already showing and something inside her felt like it was untying and loosening. Whatever it was she was enjoying it and for the first time in a long time wasn't questioning her feelings.

Before the first commercial, Goldie had fallen off to sleep. June left her on the couch worried that any uncertain movement might wake her elderly roommate and ruin her plans of wanting to stay up past the late show. She slipped off the couch and down the hall to the bathroom. Listening carefully to the Marlboro commercial and timing her bathroom trip to the sound of the commercial ending and the movie returning, June eases back on to the couch not disturbing Goldie.

The pitch of the movie was wearing on June's nerves as the tension swelled and her fingernails ached from being bitten to the quick. She reminded herself over and over that she chose to stay up and that she wanted to watch this movie in spite of the nightmares she was certain would follow. Just as the music reached its crescendo and the lizard like monster, with its bulging glass eyes crept back to its watery home, June heard two loud crashing sounds from the back yard. Jumping to her feet and running barefooted through the kitchen and out into the garage she didn't stop to think about what she was doing until her bare feet met the cold concrete floor of the garage. In the matter of a heartbeat, she ran out the side door of the garage and into the pitch darkness of the night the cool grass grabbing at her feet. Running still toward the sound forgetting her fear of the dark and being propelled by curiosity and the need to see for herself what Goldie had been suspicious of since the first of the year, that someone was stealing from her cellar, she ran around the house just as a dark shadow of a man was running into the woods behind the house. The cellar door lay flat against its stone frame silent and undisturbed but everything in June told her that it had not been that way seconds ago. She ran toward the shadow. Her mind racing in time with her feet questioning why she was doing this and not coming up with any reason to turn back. Her feet had taken on a mind of their own just as confident as she had been hours earlier in the parking lot of Patti Cake's Diner standing up to Jimbo the way she did. It was her nature to questioning herself but as fast as she was running she didn't have time to give in to her nature. The shadow was several yards ahead of her and running much faster. She wasn't sure if she meant to catch him or follow him but she kept running. Over stones and sticks and briars, her feet feeling every bit of the ground under them but she kept moving. Kept running.

She didn't feel the broken tree branch that cut across her calf slicing through her pajamas and her flesh. She didn't feel the warm sticky blood running down her leg and leaving a trail behind her. Her lungs burned with fire as she pushed on trying to match her steps to the shadows. The roaring in her ears was soon drowned out by the roar of water. It was the falls and the shadow was running directly toward the water's edge.

Focused on the dark movements ahead of her and fearing the falls, June didn't see the fallen tree. Her foot covered in blood from the gash in her calf, caught the underside of the tree, sending her tumbling head over heels over it and landing hard on the ground on the other side knocking the breath out of her.

On her back, looking up at the stars through the canopy of trees, she willed herself to breathe slowly and regain her composure. The ground soaked through her pajamas and a chill raced down her body sending a message to every cell that she was out of her element. Her legs burned with pain and she was certain she was bleeding in more than one place.

Forgetting the shadow, she put all of her attention on getting to a seated position and scanning the woods for the way out. Like waking from a dream, she felt lost and scattered scrambling for any sense of direction. Her mind told her all she had to do was get up, turn around and move in that direction but she questioned if she had actually ran in a straight line.

She knew the falls were on the far edge of the woods that separated Goldie's neighborhood in town with the ridge. She had been swimming at the falls many times but had never been there from this direction. How was she to find her way back to Goldie's? How was she to do this injured? What was she thinking tearing out from the safety of Goldie's and running after God knows who in the middle of the night and especially into the woods? Tears began to fall from her eyes. Big fat tears that didn't bother trailing down her face. Instead, these tears dove from the rims of her eyes with purpose as they splattered on her forearms covered in mud and leaves. Whoever she had become – whoever she had released from within herself when she decided to change the course of her life this afternoon and call off the wedding and move in with Goldie Filbry – whoever this person was that was standing up for herself and calling the crooked straight – was now purging the fear of a little girl from a grown woman willing to take risks.

The tears brought clarity. June raised herself up onto the fallen tree and looked toward the falls. She never heard a splash. The shadow didn't go into the water. Realizing he was still near and that she was nothing more than a sitting duck, she began to look around. Her eyes adjusted and readjusted to the darkness as she looked between each tree peering into the woods. She was looking for the shape of a man or movement.

She forced herself to listen for sounds of movement or

the sound of someone else breathing. Just as she was about to give up on being able to see anything, and knew she needed to put all of her energies into finding her way back to Goldie's, she heard the sound of a twig snapping from behind her and her blood ran cold.

"You okay?" He asked from the darkness.

The sound of his voice sliced through the night and filled her with fear that she had never experienced. She tried to still her pounding heart, to get it to slow down, to not jump out of her chest. Everything inside of her, told her, she was not in any danger. If this was the person Goldie believed it to be, she was not going to be harmed. If anything, he would be her way back to Goldie's. Still the voice from the darkness was over-whelming and frightening.

"You took a tumble." He said moving closer.

June cleared her throat and started to answer but couldn't find her voice. Again, she tried to quiet her fears with the assurance that he was not there to hurt her.

"Mind if I take a look?" He said directly behind her.

She should have been startled. Not being startled scared her more than it should have. Everything was upside down in her mind. She lost the ability to reason. She was nodding. Knowing he could see her and yet she had no idea why she was agreeing. Something about his innocent approach. The calmness in his voice. The sincerity gave her reason to believe.

As he came around in front of her, she saw him clearly and knew Goldie was right. It was Sonny Price.

"Just as I thought. You're pretty banged up." He said kneeling down in front of her and looking at her bleeding leg.

"Doesn't look like anything's broken. But you're going to have a time walking on either one of those legs for now. The one is bleeding pretty bad and the other...you're ankle...I think it may be twisted if not sprained."

June sat looking at him trying to piece together what she was supposed to do.

"You're supposed to be dead." She blurted out.

Sonny laughed under his breath. Not at what she said

but the idea of it.

"You think it's funny? Everyone in town. Everyone! Thinks you're dead."

"That's the way I planned it." He said as he continued looking her over for broken bones.

"Well, you might have planned it better."

June's naïve honesty caught Sonny off guard and he fell back on his heels wanting to laugh but thought better of it.

"You don't say? So what should I have planned better?"

"Well for starters. You shouldn't have stolen from Mrs. Filbry. Once was a mistake. But to keep doing it. Over and over again. That was stupid."

Laughing now, Sonny found a clear place on the ground in front of June, pulled out a pack of cigarettes and lit one.

"What makes you think I was stealing from her?" He offered a cigarette to June and she shook her head no.

"Why else would you be sneaking into her cellar? Besides, she said you're stealing from her and I'd rather take the word of a Sunday school teacher any day over a man that runs out on his family and hides in the woods for six months stealing from an old women."

June saw the expression on Sonny's face change and she immediately regretted her newfound boldness. This was something she was going to have to learn how to tame like her natural curls and the ruby lipstick from the Avon samples.

"Now you just hold on missy. You don't need to go around passing judgment on folks you don't know. Especially when you don't have enough sense to go running after things in the dark. Just look at you. You're so banged up and bruised I could leave you here for the wolves to eat. How would you like that?"

"There ain't no wolves around here."

"Be careful what you think you know little sister. There's plenty of wolves in this world. Plenty."

June swallowed hard realizing he wasn't talking about the four-legged furry kind. She was in over her head and she was sitting in the dark, in the woods, talking with a dead man. How was this going to look if anyone knew? How would she explain this one?

"I'm sorry. I shouldn't have said that. I've been saying a lot of things lately that I just don't know where they are coming from. Just haven't been myself. Believe me when I say it's not like me to run out into the woods. Day or night."

Tears, slow and salty, began to run down June's face. Sonny saw them long before she felt them. Embarrassed, June tucked her chin to her chest and resigned herself to whatever came next. She was all out of steam and her newfound gumption had left her cold and wet and lost.

"Listen. I'll make you a deal." Sonny waited for her to acknowledge that she was listening. The slight slump of her shoulders was indication enough that she was.

"No one has to know you ran out into the woods. No one has to know you ran after me. Like you said, everyone, well almost everyone, thinks I'm dead. So, there's no reason, unless you can think of one, to bring this up."

Waiting for her to begin to show interest in his proposal, Sonny gave his words time to take root. June looked up through her sweat soaked curls and waited for him to finish.

"You can't make it back to the edge of the woods on your own but I think once you get to the edge, you can make it back to the house." She nodded in agreement. "Okay then, I'll carry you back." She hesitated. "It's the least I can do. And once you get back, if you want to venture out and tell Mrs. Filbry or anyone else you saw me tonight, well then, I leave that up to you and your conscience. But if not, then we are as good as strangers that met in the night and that's that. What do you say?"

"But what about the stealing? Are you going to stop the stealing?"

"I'm not stealing."

"But she said you are. I don't think she would lie."

Sonny exhaled loudly. "It wasn't me but I know who it was and I'll take care of it. Take care of him."

"Think about it. If you really want to do something good. You should think about going back to your own home.

To your wife and little girl. Forget this business of righting some wrong no matter who or what the problem is."

Suddenly, in her mind, June saw Jimbo standing on Sonny and Kathleen's front porch, like so many times over the last few months. Doing his job as it had been assigned to him, all because the man that was now sitting in front of her, in the woods, decided one day to turn tail and run.

"You know there are a lot of people wondering what happened to you. And, these same people are taking care of your wife and baby."

"You sound like you know someone in particular that's doing this."

"As a matter of fact, I do. He was going to be my husband until this afternoon."

"What a minute. Are you saying my wife has taken up with your..."

"No! I ain't saying nothing of the sort. You're confusing two different situations. It's his job. Or at least that's what he says. And, before you question that too, I believe him. He has been asked by the sheriff to watch out for her, but I'm telling you, I believe what he is really being asked to do, is watch out for you!"

Sonny wasn't surprised by what June shared. He had his suspicions from seeing Bishop at his place over the last few months. June confirmed it.

"Yeah, I've seen him there. But how does that play into you not marrying him? What? You don't love him?"

"I love him. I just can't see marrying him. I don't expect it to make sense. Not to you or anyone else."

"It makes sense. Not that I could explain it any better than you have, but I get it."

Adjusting his legs to a more comfortable position and studying June's ankle a bit more and seeing the swelling had abated, Sonny offers again to help her to the wood's edge.

"So, we are in agreement?" Sonny asked steadying June to walk the remaining few yards to Goldie's back door.

"Yeah, we are in agreement. I didn't see you and you didn't see me."

"Agreed."

"Well, you take care stranger."

"Yeah, you take care too ghost."

June hobbled to the backdoor, across the cold cement garage floor and through the opened kitchen door, as she had left it. The sun would soon be breaking open the morning sky like a yolk pouring from a broken shell, and she knew she needed to get inside and tend to her leg and ankle.

The TV had been turned off, the popcorn bowl and Dr. Pepper bottle had been removed from the coffee table and Goldie was sound asleep in her bed. June showered and wrapped her scraped leg with a clean bandage and helped herself to the kitchen once again. This time she prepared French toast for her generous roommate while rehearsing her response if she got the third degree.

Chapter Twenty-seven

That old familiar feeling crept up Sonny's spine seeping out through his spinal column and out into every nerve ending. It filled him with dread and hope at the same time. His time was limited. Most days he felt like every minute of the day squeezed in on him, reminding him not to waste any second of the precious time he had been given. The guilt was growing heavier. The guilt from wasting precious time.

He was born with this sense of dread and hope. He dreaded the last grain of sand that would soon fall from the hourglass God had issued him. He thought of the angelic being that was in charge of counting the grains of sand as they tumbled thoughtless and sometimes carelessly into the pyramid of his life. He wanted to bargain with him, knowing he couldn't bargain with God, to slow the pace, to stop the spillage, to give him more – time.

He was filled with hope too. Each morning was a hopeful reminder that it would end soon. Whatever day of trouble he found himself in, he knew from the lessons his limited time had taught him, that everything passed in its own time and things never lasted as long as the dread that preceded them.

He knew this was a gift of wisdom that had been given to him but was unsure of its giver. He told himself it was from his father. A father he never knew except from offhanded comments others made usually in times of trouble or concern for Sonny's wellbeing. Well intentioned comments from kind-hearted people that only wanted what was best for him not knowing they were filling him with shame and doubt for being a boy without a father.

Time was squeezing in. Pushing against him. Reminding him to act. He had a choice to make. He had to return to Kathleen and the baby and begin again. Or he had to leave Mud Flats. Leave Scots Ridge, his home, and never return. After running into June last night, he knew his absence would once again be on the minds and agendas of people that mattered. People like Sheriff Ruskin Bright and Deputy Jimbo Bishop. People like Goldalena Filbry and Florence Bright. And people like June and Kathleen. They all wanted to put the pieces of the puzzle together. Fit them together nicely and neatly and call things done. Finished and complete.

Sonny wanted to be the kind of man that did things on account of someone else. To put others before his own needs but he never found that part of himself. It had been locked up tight down deep within him or never there to begin with. Whatever the reason. Whatever the cause. Sonny Price was not a man to put anyone before his own needs. No one would ever call him selfish. At least not to his face. But he knew it. He knew the only thing to call what he was feeling was selfishness. It had taken him twenty plus years of living with it to come face to face with it and give it a name.

The screen door slammed and pushed Sonny's thoughts away from himself and to the sound of work boots stomping across the side yard. Chickens squawked as Arvis cussed.

"Boy! You still laying in the bed? If you ain't feeling poorly then I 'spect you need to be about it. Got things to do. Ain't got time to lay about." Arvis stood at the hood of the truck calling. Rousing the sleeping hound dogs and Sonny.

Sonny slid off the open tailgate and into the cool morning air. The sun had not lifted its head above the horizon leaving the holler in ghostly purple shadows.

"Morning." Sonny stretched to his full height. The dogs stretched long and groaned as their tight muscles gave way.

"Won't be for long. Got plenty to do today. Time is wasting." Arvis said handing Sonny the shovel he had pulled from the pile of tools and scrap wood from the yard. How Arvis knew where anything was in the massive junk yard he called home was anyone's guess, but he could take a man to anything in question and pull it from its hiding place. Old broken down appliances and household furnishings competed for space among piles of scrap wood and metal. Electrical cords draped like a spider's web overhead supplying current to drop cords and extension cords for power tools. A fire burned day and night under a cast iron kettle used to clean meat of various kinds. Not too far from it was another cast iron kettle kept nearly frozen over with chunks of ice the size of a man's arm floating in water. Sonny had spent his fair share of time sitting in the heat of the boiling water or just about frost bit from the icy water, each with its purpose in skinning and cleaning everything from chickens to possums and the implements to get the job done.

Just the mention of wasting time set Sonny's frayed nerves on edge, as he gritted his teeth to keep his tongue from costing him a hiding place. He didn't like owing anyone anything and he especially didn't like being obliged to Arvis Ange, but like it or not, he owed the man plenty keeping his whereabouts quiet for months and for giving him a place to sleep and food for his belly.

"Whatya got for me today?" Sonny tried to sound interested but Arvis wasn't buying it. He could smell fear before it filled a man's pores and could see doubt before it had time to slide across a man's mind. He also wasn't a man to take to compliments or false praise. Sonny wanted to show his appreciation but he knew the only way to do that was to bend to his benefactor's demands. Do the work and do it without question. That was the means of praise or payment he could offer.

"I've got a mess of fish over yonder. They'll need cleaning. They was biting good last night so I just kept reeling them in." Sonny nodded realizing he wasn't aware that Arvis had been out all night fishing. He wondered if Arvis knew he had been at the river last night too. He wondered too if Arvis had seen Tinkum's campsite upon the bluff. And, it he had, if he saw Tinkum too.

"Alright. I can handle that. What else you got?" Sonny asked.

Arvis laughed at the boy's eagerness and pride. "Got a bucket of nails that need straightening." Arvis pointed to a keg of nails and watched as the realization spread across Sonny's face.

"Alright. I'll take care of that. Guess I can find a hammer in the tool barn." Sonny knew he'd be all day looking for a hammer in the tool barn but wanted to show he had figured his way around the place and didn't want to draw attention to the obviousness of the scattering of tools lying about the yard. He was forever bruising his ankles and shins the first few days he was staying at Ange's, accidently stepping on hammers and rolling his ankle or bruising his shin with an ax handle.

Arvis was enjoying this a bit too much and decided he would see just how far he could go with this, "And while you're at it, reckon I'll get you to move the outhouse."

Without blinking an eye or showing any signs of being disagreeable, Sonny said alright and put his hand up over his eyes as if to shade them from the sun that had yet to rise above the hills, and looked around for a new location for the outhouse.

Arvis laughed to himself satisfied in what he had started and knew Sonny was just like his daddy had been and given enough room and the right amount of nudging, and the boy, like his daddy before him, would do the right thing. Until then, there'd be plenty of chores to help pave the way.

"Alright then, I reckon you've got enough to get you started this morning. You get done with that and come see me. There's plenty we need to get done before the sun sets." Arvis looked to the hill where the sun had decided to blink over the edge hearing its name, as Sonny marched off to the kettle to skim the top and begin cleaning the knives for the fish.

Dipping the knives into the steaming water to clean them, Sonny sat with his legs wrapped around an upturned stone and laying the fish one at time upon it, he cleaned and fileted them.

Arvis wrestled out ten Styrofoam coolers from the bed of his truck and several blocks of ice from the well house for Sonny to use to store the cleaned fish. It was his intention to take the fish in to town and sell to the first church with a car in its parking lot or to the Masonic Lodge. Either one would be having a fish fry to raise money sooner or later and would need fish for the frying.

Filling the coolers with a layer of ice, Arvis studied Sonny out of the corner of his eye. The boy was the spitting image of his daddy. A daddy, Arvis knew, the boy had never known and also knew his mama mourned for to the day she died. To grow up without a word spoke about the man that gave you life had to be the most sorrowful way to live, Arvis thought. It was no wonder the boy had ran away at the first signs of being a father himself. How was he to know how to be something no one had taught him how to be? Arvis knew Ephraim had done his best. They were all there together in the beginning, Arvis, Ephraim, Henry and Tinkum but only Arvis was there in the end. This morning, as the sun eased down into the holler like a lost child, Arvis decided to go on with the plan he made last night while fishing on the river, to tell the boy his history. Maybe then, if he knew, he would make the best choice for himself and his family. Maybe he could overcome his accidental legacy.

Chapter Twenty-eight

"Your daddy was left-handed too." Arvis said stopping to draw attention to the way Sonny was holding the fileting knife. Sonny slid the knife down the length of the fish with the ease of a surgeon. He kept up the speed of his work mindful of what lay ahead of him for the day and knowing too the best way to keep Arvis entertained was to leave him to whatever he had on his mind.

"I knew all your daddy's people but I reckon he was the only southpaw among them. Almost fitting you'd be one too. I was sweet on your Aunt Caroline. Reckon we'd a married if she hadn't got so sick. Lord, I guess it's been nearly thirty years since she passed. Some days it seems like yesterd'y. Same way with your daddy. Seems like just yesterd'y me and him and Ephraim was boys thinking we was men. Working fields all day and chasing women all night." Arvis snorted. Sonny stopped his work long enough to let the image build in his mind realizing he wasn't that different from his daddy or the man that was sitting across from him. Arvis reared back in the cane bottom chair, leaning it against the fender well of his pickup truck and gave way to his mind tugging him back in time.

"Oh my sweet Caroline. If only she'd 'a lived. What a life we'd had. But too many leave us too soon. Your mama left too soon too. I surely do miss them both. Last time I saw them we were altogether. Ram and Milly, Tinkum and your mama, and me and Caroline. Course that was before anybody was thinking on marrying. We was just kids but we had paired off like every living creature does. Can't say it was love at first sight for anyone else but I'm telling you it was love at first sight for me. There was never a prettier creature on this God's green earth than Caroline Elizabeth Gentry and there never will be. Why God took her the way He did is not for me to wonder and I suppose the same can be said for your mama."

Sonny was finished cleaning the fish. He had cleaned the knives in the hot water and dried them. Leaving them to sharpen later, he decided to rest a minute or two and listen while Arvis reminisced. He was curious about what he had to say about his daddy considering this was already more than anyone had ever said about him in all his growing up years.

"Your daddy had heard that the railroad was laying tracks down near the Alabama line, so he decided to go off down there and see about getting him a job laying track. He hadn't worked a day in his life doing anything but farming but he figured work was work and he was ready to lay his hand to something other than a plow. It didn't take much to convince me to go along and nothing could pursued Ephraim from leaving Fulton and Milly. So off the two of us went on foot. We hitched a ride when we could and I guess it was when we got to just the other side of Nashville that I decided I had enough of this adventure and turned around and came back. Well, your daddy was too stubborn to turn around. So, to spite us all, he kept to his plan and went on down to see about working for the rail-road.

I'll never forget to the day I die the look on your mama's face when I told her that he had gone off to find work. I was the longest trying to figure out if she was mad at me for not staying with him knowing how his hot temper and short wick could get him into trouble or if she was mad at your daddy for leaving her behind." Arvis paused. The floodgate of memories washing through him.

Sonny's attention was drawn to the massive bull in the pasture. Its white face like a mask hiding its thoughts. He envied the beast's stoic expression.

Arvis lifted his sweat stained bib cap. Scratched the oily patch of steal colored hair on his head and refitted the cap. "It was about this time, while Tinkum was trying to be in both places at the same time. He'd work a while down yonder and then come back to town only to run back to where the money was good. It was about then that the creeks got up. We had rain nearly every day for going on three months. Back then, I didn't know a soul that wasn't dealing with a flooded field or a house with three or four foot of standing water. It was bad. Bad for a long time. Your mama took sick sometime before the water got up. I don't know whose idea it was, and I don't rightly know if it matters, but your mama's twin sister came to stay with your mama and daddy. I know people have talked saying if your daddy had stayed put and not been high footing it out of town every chance he got things would have been different. But, I'm telling you I was there and I don't care what anyone says, he did the best he could do. They both did."

Arvis sat quietly for a while. Sonny wasn't sure if he was finished talking. If he had talked himself into a stupor or if he was reliving events too hard to put into words. He understood that feeling. He knew if it hadn't been for the old gypsy woman understanding him as well as she did without him knowing the words to put to his thoughts and feelings, he would be lost in a world of silence. A cold chill ran through him like slippery eels. The look on the old man's face told the tale.

"Let me just tell you Sonny-boy, a man can live with a lot of misery but losing the woman he loves is a deep abiding sorrow I wouldn't wish on my worst enemy."

Sonny was lost. Was Arvis still talking about Tinkum or had his thoughts shifted back to Caroline and his own love lost. Sonny knew what it was like to live with loss. He watched for days as Kathleen lay in their bed, day and night, lost in her sadness and there was nothing he could do to bring her back. She was trapped. He was trapped too.

Pulling a cigarette from his breast pocket, Sonny smoked it piecing together the story, his life story, Arvis had piled on him. The cigarette once burning with life lay cold and used up between his feet. He reached instinctively into his breast pocket for another but the pack was empty save for a piece long missing its filtered end. He touched the broken bud to his moist lips and its dry paper took hold. Closing his lips around it, he lit the end and sucked the life out of it drawing the warm smoke into his lungs to feel something, anything but the dull ache of his head and piercing pain in his chest.

"Yours was an accidental legacy. Your daddy lost just about everything to the floodwater. Everything had changed in the blink of an eye. He couldn't live another day twisted up with the idea that he had lost your mama. Yep that's right. Your mama, the woman that gave you life, died in the flood. The woman you've known as your mama was your mama's twin sister." Arvis spit a long stream of tobacco juice from his mouth, wiped his face with the back of his hand and cleaned any trace of tobacco spittle and guilt from his face. The weight of his life, had been lifted. Sonny knew his past and it was up to him now to piece together what was left of it. It was up to him to do with it what he chose.

Looking at his pocket watch Arvis pitched forward in his chair, "Well, enough reminiscing, we both got work to do. I'm going to take this fish into town and leave you to it. Want me to get you some cigarettes while I'm there?"

He didn't wait for an answer knowing he would get the cigarettes anyway and by now Sonny wasn't in the mood to answer anyone about anything. Leaving Arvis to load the fish on his truck by himself, Sonny walked off toward the tool barn to find a hammer.

Chapter Twenty-nine

Sweat rolled off Sonny's forehead missing his eyes and dripping onto the tree stump he was using to hammer the bent nails straight. His knuckles were swollen from gripping the hammer and nails and from suffering misjudged blows from the hammer. Lost in thought and decision, he played back everything Arvis had said. His stomach growled reminding him for the second time in the day that he had not eaten.

With two coffee cans filled with straightened nails and the keg not showing any signs that it had been disturbed, he made his first decision of the day and stopped long enough to eat something to stave off the hunger for a few more hours. Helping himself to the deep freeze that leaned more than it should on the uneven ground, its long black cord reaching up to meet one of the extension cords crisscrossed overhead, he found a box of ice cream sandwiches and found a cool spot under a walnut tree. With his mason jar filled from the well, he ate one ice cream sandwich after another thoughtless that he was eating the whole box.

Sonny washed the sweetness from his mouth and let the cold well water fill his stomach pushing out any room for hunger. His mind ran down through time from his father and his losses, to himself and all that he had lost. He was taking a personal inventory, when like someone standing behind him whispering in his ear, he realized he had not lost anything, not yet. That all he had in this life was still his. That unlike his daddy and the choices he made in his life, he still had time. And it was that last thought. The realization that time was no longer working against him, that Sonny knew what he had to do.

* * *

Across town Arvis was unloading his coolers of catfish as Goldie Filbry slowly filled in the church's check with her nearly illegible chicken scratch while she read aloud each word as she worked, "Paid to the order of Arvis E. Ange. You do use your middle initial don't you Arvis or should I spell out Eugene?"

"E will be sufficient Goldie." Arvis grumbled exasperated by the woman's need to draw out any given moment in time to her liking with no thought to a man needing to be on about his business. How Henry put up with her stubbornness all those years was beyond him.

"E it is then. Paid to the order of Arvis E. Ange. In the amount of ten dollars. You know Arvis ten dollars for a mess of fish not knowing just how many you have tucked in under all that ice is a pretty steep price if you ask me." Goldie said. And just as Arvis was about to inform Goldie that no one had asked her that he had made the deal with the preacher and that it was her sole responsibility to make out the check and that's where it ended, she added. "But no one asked me." Then blew on the check to dry the ink and with the same motion to shoo flies she handed him the check.

"I don't reckon in all your running you've laid eyes on the Price boy have you?" Goldie asked without asking pretending to be preoccupied with filling in the check registry and demonstrating the prowess her particular office of church treasury demanded.

"Nope, can't say I've seen him on my routes but then again, I believe I've already answered you on this matter before." Arvis said sliding his greased filled thumbnail down the folded edge of the check and then tucking it into his billfold.

"I know what you've said. And, I know how you said it. I just thought I'd give you a chance to think over your past answer and answer me again but seems to me you only know one way of talking." Goldie wrapped her fingers under the edge of the large black leather binder that held the church's checks and hugged it to her. Tapping the toe of her penny loafer with its empty space where the penny should be, she waited for Arvis to reconsider his answer. After all they were standing in the parking lot of the church and as far as Goldie was concerned it was just as sacred as the being on the inside. If Arvis was willing to offer up his brand of lies in the parking lot he would be just as inclined if she took in to the middle of the baptistery waters.

"Arvis Eugene Ange, as long as I live, I'll never understand a liar. Give a man the opportunity to tell the truth, as my dearly departed husband would say, and a good man will never disappoint you. What do you think that says for you?" Goldie leaned forward giving purpose to her words.

Arvis laughed at the sight of Goldie wearing her dead husband's Sunday suit and resurrecting the good judge in the church parking lot with her poor admonition of the scripture. "It makes me late. That's what it makes me. You've got your fish for your fund raiser and I've got my check." And with the quick tug on the brim of his cap, Arvis crawled into his pickup truck and pulled out of the parking lot leaving Goldie just as curious as he found her.

Circling the Square a couple of times to shake her off his trail if she had decided to follow him and then deciding to take a run out by the state line to see a man about a litter of pups, Arvis was good as gone before Goldie had made her mind up what to do next.

Torn between following Arvis or going home to see what June was up to, she decided to leave Arvis alone for the time being and turned her Buick in the direction of home.

* * *

With a blanket spread out on the grass, the straps of her swim suit laying loose along her sides and the radio resting against the screen of the open bedroom window, June didn't hear the car door slam or the heavy footsteps of Goldie coming through the house surveying the place as she came in one door and out the other.

"You're burning. Might want to turn over or get in the shade for a while. Have you ate?" Goldie said standing at the edge of the blanket.

June grabbed her swimsuit straps and quickly tied them across her tender sunburnt back as she sat up. Feeling suddenly insecure about laying out. She jumped to her feet and started folding the blanket pulling the corners together and spilling her suntan lotion and magazines onto the grass.

"You don't have to come in on my account. But by the looks of your back, you may be in some pain tonight." Goldie looked toward the radio up in the bedroom window. "Now that's clever."

June smiled thinking she was being paid a compliment and it somehow eased the sting of her embarrassment and the sunburn.

"Guess I lost track of how long I've been out here. I do that sometimes." June said as she gathered up her things and followed Goldie into the house. Going on to the bedroom where she was staying, she turned off the radio and put it back on the nightstand beside her bed.

"Bologna or ham?" Goldie called out from the kitchen.

June answered either was fine with her as she came back into the kitchen and sat at the small Formica table at the place setting laid out for her.

"Well, I'm having bologna and cheese. Mustard?" Goldie asked.

"Yes ma'am mustard is fine." June said inspecting the raised pink skin along her waist.

"You know June, you can have whatever you like. Just let me know and if I don't have it we can go to the store and get it." Goldie said sensing June's discomfort.

June appreciated how the old woman had a way of defusing the air around her. Feeling the hint of shame grabbing at her heels, June was ready for a tongue-lashing or worse the silent treatment but instead she was met with compassion. She had been used to being misunderstood and expected the rest of the world operated the same way. Jimbo was constantly getting frustrated with her reaction to his easy going response to things and tried to convince her that the world was not as dark and ugly as she thought, but that was one boy's opinion and she couldn't trust what little she suspected he knew. But she felt she could trust Mrs. Filbry. She was as old as her parents and had been married to a judge. Surely if she said it was so, it was so, and that was good enough for June. At least for now.

"So, what have you been doing this morning except laying on the grass in your bathing suit? Can't you swim? Or don't you want to? You too old for the swimming pool at the park now? I guess I can understand that. How's your sandwich? I got some lemonade or I can make us some tea. Which you want?" Goldie said not giving time between questions for answers.

June didn't know which question to answer first.

"Cat got your tongue? What did you do for breakfast? I'm sorry I was up and out before you were up. Guess I'll have to get used to having someone in the house. I had some cold biscuit pudding in the refrigerator. You could have helped yourself to some of that for breakfast or made yourself some of that fancy toast, you're so fond of. My guess is your mama either had you in the kitchen at an early age or kept you out of the kitchen all together. Mamas tend to be from one extreme to the other. Nothing in between when it comes to women and their kitchens."

Again, June sat still, only her jaw moving chewing her bologna sandwich, choosing not to answer the long list of questions being hurled at her.

Once Goldie sat down with a glass of lemonade in front of both of them, she filled her mouth with bologna instead of questions.

June feeling as though Goldie's eyes were still asking the questions, tried her best to answer each one as best she could remember, beginning at the end and working backwards.

With a hard swallow, she said, "Mama never said one way or the other about me being in the kitchen. Guess that was her way of giving permission. Not saying anything at all. I watched and learned and once I started doing she stopped. At least as far as I could tell she stopped. No point in two people rolling out biscuit dough or cutting a chicken in parts. Not that we helped one another. I guess once I started cooking she just left me to it. I'd come in of the afternoons from school and start supper. By the time I was old enough to be gone off with my friends on the weekends, she was back to doing most of the cooking. I wish I could say we cooked together. Maybe some girls have that kind of time with their mamas but not me. "June said between bites.

June took a bite of her sandwich and thought of the other things she didn't share with her mother. Like sewing and canning and things a girl should learn from her mother. But those were not the things Goldie had asked and there was no point talking about things that couldn't be changed.

"I wasn't hungry when I woke up and the pool tends to be too full this time of the day. The older kids usually wait until later in the afternoon before going if they go at all. We've been going to the river to swim for ages."

Goldie's eyebrows shot up full of questions but her mouth was too full of bologna and cheese to ask and still be lady-like.

"It's safe. The county has cleared out a place shallow enough to swim. It's more like swimming in a lake than river. The water is almost still. So that's where I'd been today had I still been with Jimbo but I kinda feel odd about going down there right now so soon after our break up or postponement or whatever this is supposed to be."

Feeling the heat rise to the surface of her sunburnt face June decided to avoid any further conversation about Jimbo and their fragile relationship. It wasn't doing her any good and it really was none of Mrs. Filbry's business. She doubted the old woman was the least bit interested in what she and Jimbo had planned. So leaving that subject alone was satisfying for both of them as far as she could tell.

"I think that pretty much covers it. I believe you're right. I think I'm going to really be feeling this sunburn tonight." June gently rubbed her bare shoulders and it was then she realized she had sat at Mrs. Filbry's kitchen table eating a sandwich wearing nothing but her swimsuit. If her mama and daddy could see her now they would think she had forgotten every decent thing they had taught her. Never in a hundred years would she have ever come to her mama and daddy's table dressed as she was but then again as she looked across the table at Mrs. Filbry dressed in a fine blue seersucker suit that rivaled anything in the window of men's store on the Square, she doubted they would have appreciated that either.

"I reckon you covered just about everything." Goldie said taking a long swallow of lemonade to wash down her sandwich. Eyeing June through the bottom of the glass and seeing no reason not to continue the conversation Goldie shared that she had spent the morning running errands in town and that she had just come from the church.

"Bought some fish from Arvis Ange for the fish fry. You planning on going to the fish fry, I hope."

June nodded certain Goldie was not really asking for a response expecting her to attend whether she planned on it now or later.

"That man has a way about him." Goldie paused thinking about the best direction to take with what she wanted to say. June curious to know what she was thinking but also feeling the chill of being indoors and out of the sun thought it best to change into something more substantial than her swimsuit.

"Excuse me Mrs. Filbry, but before I catch a chill I think I better get on some clothes. Can I clean this up for you?" Goldie shooed June away from the table just as they both heard a knock at the front door and the sound of Florence Bright calling out to them as she came through the living room.

Chapter Thirty

"What are you two up to today?" Florence asked as she rounded the kitchen door from the living room. Her face as bright as her enthusiasm and as sunburnt as June's

"Looks to me like you and June are both sporting a nice sunburn. You been out in the yard today?" Goldie cut through the niceties. Florence and June looked at each other comparing each other's sunburn.

"Got some cold cream in my bedroom. Guess I best get some on me before this goes to stinging." June let her words trail behind her as she made her way down the hall and away from the two older women.

"You been out running errands this morning?" Florence asked as she made herself comfortable at the kitchen table.

Goldie pulled a glass from the cabinet and poured Florence some lemonade.

"Been over to the church. Bought a mess of catfish from Arvis Ange for the fish fry on Friday. Reckon I can count on you and Ruskin to attend."

Ruskin and Florence attended the Presbyterian Church on the Square but was always ready to support the other local congregations with their fundraisers.

"Sure. Ruskin loves a good fish fry. Y'all raising money for something in particular?" Florence asked raising her glass of lemonade and taking a long sip.

Goldie shooed the question away not wanting to get into a protracted conversation about money being raised for something she had little to no interest in especially when she had more pressing matters on her mind. Picking up from where her thoughts left off.

"I asked him if he knew anything about Sonny Price." Goldie said.

"Him? Who? Mr. Ange?" Florence was confused in the circling conversation.

Goldie nodded, "And, he gave me the same dang fired answer he gave me the last time I asked him."

"What did you expect?"

Waving her hand again as if to shoo away Florence's comments and her unrealistic expectations that Ange would suddenly decide to tell the truth, Goldie dropped her head like a buzzard studying road kill and pressed her point.

"I tell you what I expect. I expect to be the one to find Sonny Price and send him packing back to his wife. I know in my bones that Arvis Ange has something to do with this. Arvis has a debt to pay and he's been most his life waiting for the opportunity to pay it. I know it. And, he knows, I know it!"

Florence nearly choked on her lemonade as she waited for Goldie to finish her story. Her eyes set on Goldie's pleading for the widow to continue. If Goldie doubted Florence's interest before, she had no reason to doubt now with Florence struck spellbound.

"The judge and I were courting around this time. He hadn't been lawyering for long and we were making plans to marry come spring. I wrestled with the thoughts of marrying him. Looking back now I can see better why my heart kept pulling in his direction but at the time all I could see was his bruised ego from returning to the ridge instead of staying in Nashville to practice law. Said he never intended to be a small town lawyer and planned on heading back to Nashville as soon as he had enough money and experience. I think if it hadn't been for the trouble that followed he would have kept true to his word and I'd been married to someone else." Goldie fell silent caught in the emotion of her memories.

"Trouble? What trouble? I don't recall you ever saying there was trouble between the two of you?" Florence said eager to know more.

"Weren't no trouble of our making, but it was trouble all the same." Goldie said.

Goldie sat quietly for a moment or two lost in thought and the long road memory tends to take. She was finding her way back to the place and time that had been eating at her ever since she heard about the car accident and Sonny Price missing.

"It was all over cards. That's how they decided it. It was the four of them. My Henry was among them. They'd been drinking and playing cards for all of a weekend. The rain had ran them out of the fields and time was creeping up on them wearing on their minds and stealing their common sense. One of them pulled out a deck of cards. Seems like I remember Henry saying Tinkum always had a deck of cards on him. They were all stove up from not earning their pay that day due to the rain and not wanting to go too far from the field, they found shelter in the hay barn. With the doors thrown open they could keep an eye on the skies and the field and the road. Nothing like getting caught off guard when you're doing something that could eventually bring you shame. Least ways that's how I imagine it." Goldie said twisting the end with her special brand of contempt.

"Henry said they had been playing going on two maybe three hours and were getting tired of hearing the rain beat the tin roof and rush off the eaves when Sonny's daddy raised the stakes."

Sitting on the edge of her chair, Florence knew the story was about to get good and poured herself another glass of lemonade watching the story break fresh across Goldalena's face.

"Said, they had played for pennies, nickels and dimes when Tinkum offered up an opportunity."

"Opportunity?" Florence asked between sips of lemonade.

Goldie nodded letting the idea take shape. She poured the last of the lemonade in her glass, took a long sip and picked up where she left off.

"Tinkum said he was going down near the Alabama state line to work for the railroad. Said there was big money to be made there and he was going to get his share. Henry said he had no intentions of moving anywhere but back to Nashville so this was no opportunity for him. Besides, Henry was quick to point out that raising the stakes with an opportunity of money was not as good as the money itself. Well, that got Tinkum all riled up.

He said, he would bet them all that he'd make more in a month, than they had made all year, and wagered his son for it."

"Son! You mean Sonny? But, I thought this was before any of y'all had gotten married?" Florence said trying to keep her voice down from the pure shock of what she was hearing.

Goldie nodded and waved her hand as if to tap down Florence's reaction.

"It was. It was. That's what I'm telling you. That's what makes this whole thing as ugly as sin itself. Henry said they played another hand, none of them expecting things to turn out the way they did. How were they to know?" Goldie grew quiet and her expression and mood turned dark and somber as she revealed the sobering truth behind Tinkum's bet.

"It wasn't no time before the events of that rainy afternoon took shape and began haunting those that remained. You see, Tinkum went off to work for the railroad and that was the last anyone heard of him, as best I know. Word was he got off down there and forgot all about what he left behind. But I believe, it was that bet he made, his life for his son's. Now, Henry and Ephraim and Arvis knew something was up with Tinkum. He was never one to walk the straight and narrow. So when Olive came around telling them of her troubles, they put two and two together and realized Tinkum knew the day of the card game he had no intentions of coming back. It was Arvis that won that hand of cards and it was Arvis that decided then that he would be responsible for the boy but Olive wouldn't have anything to do with their bet. She was determined to take care of things herself but she was as prideful as Tinkum and we all knew she couldn't manage. She had just lost her twin sister to the flood after taking care of her for months from the diphtheria and now she was raising her sister's son by herself."

It was Ephraim that set her up in the house beside him and Mildred. Between him and Arvis and Henry she didn't want for a thing. Time passed and the boy grew up not knowing his daddy. As time went on, Ephraim and Mildred had a house full so what was one more. Sonny grew up under the shadow of the Hatch children and Henry did what he could to make sure his needs were met too. Everyone did their part feeling responsible for that afternoon of playing cards." Goldie said looking exhausted from the release of loosening a lifetime of secrets.

Florence was stunned not knowing where to begin asking the laundry list of questions crowding her mind. "So tell me, why then are you so determined that Sonny is alive and do you think he has been the one getting in to your cellar? I guess I've misunderstood. I've been thinking you wanted Ruskin to arrest him."

Goldie blushed at the thought of her actions not matching her intentions. Her anger at the situation, its festering over time, had caused her true intentions to be misunderstood. She felt she would forever be asking God to help her with her anger.

"I want him back at his home with his wife and child. It burns me to no end that he is out running the roads or hiding in one of them caves up on the bluffs somewhere not taking responsibility for his life and those that rely on him. I just don't want him repeating the life his father lived. That boy never knew his daddy yet that man's blood courses through his veins and pumps through his heart. It has influenced him in ways he will never know. But he also had others helping him grow and sadly we were not able to give him the love and care his daddy should have given him. If anything, I suppose I'm angry at myself for not doing enough. For not letting Henry be more involved in the boy's life." Goldie said.

Laughing she thinks about what she is saying and the release confession gives. "Listen at me calling him a boy. He is a full-grown man. And that's how he should be living. Like a grown man and not some boy running around in the woods too scared of his shadow to face life. Arvis is involved. I know he is. He is just as guilt ridden as I am about the whole mess. We've watched over that boy, man, all his born days and to know he is out there somewhere and we can't bring him home. We can't let him know he has a family among us that have watched over him. Loved him. Well, that just breaks my heart."

Florence and Goldie sit soaking in the emotions that welled up not aware that June had been listening from the bedroom.

Believing she could do something about this June quickly made her way down the hall, mumbled some excuse for leaving the house and hurried out the back door and across the yard to the woods.

Chapter Thirty-one

The moon competed with the leafy canopy of the woods pushing its light down into the murky darkness. June regretted leaving Goldie's unprepared. She had waited in the woods for most of the afternoon for any possible sighting of Sonny. Why she thought he would come back to where she had seen him before, just because she was sitting there expecting it, only served as a constant reminder to her that she was as naïve as Jimbo said.

His voice had become the voice of her conscience trading places with her daddy and now he berated her over the ill-advised notion of sitting in the middle of the woods where no one knew she was there. Especially waiting for someone that everyone believed to be dead.

Back and forth June's mind switched gears on whether she should stay or go. She tried to recite all the reasons why she was there in the first place. She was there to help. She knew if she could talk to Sonny again, maybe just maybe, she could convince to go home. She could tell him about that story Goldie told Florence and he would be just as moved as she was and he would know the right thing to do was to go home and quit roaming the woods. The woods she was sitting in alone.

But, if he wasn't there, then did that mean he wasn't roaming the woods. Did it mean Goldie got it all wrong? Could someone, anyone, be wrong for a lifetime, or more? June's mind questioned whether she had really seen him in the woods the last time or did she dream it. Immediately she doused the idea that it was a dream. She knew she saw him. She knew he was alive. And, she knew that he wanted to go home. She just knew it.

Just like she knew, she truly wanted to go home. She appreciated all that Mrs. Filbry was doing giving her a place to stay that wasn't too far out of the way so that she could refocus her thoughts on what was best for her future. She was beginning to believe Mrs. Filbry's advice that sometimes people need to get away from the familiar to see what they had was all they needed.

June thought the same for Sonny. For whatever reason he felt he couldn't go home after his wreck. After he faked his death, he really just wanted to go home. The woods or wherever he had been was just far enough away for him to see home more clearly and to know home was where he belonged.

The cool night air was little comfort to her badly sunburned skin. June needed to get some relief from the burning. Walking out into the water on the bluff of the river, she decided to ease into the slow current staying clear of the channel and cool her skin.

Stepping out onto the flat limestone, she watched as the water, nearly ankle deep, rushed over her bare feet. Moss danced in the rushing water and caught the moon's light. It was beautiful and June felt compelled to reach down and touch it, to let it run over her hand. She knew this could be tricky. One misstep and she would be upside down on the flat overhang. Almost a three-story drop off to the water below would be the only thing to break her fall. That is if she missed the jutting shelves of rock on the way down to waiting reserve.

Easing down to a seated position, she decided to give herself the best option for touching the moss and still stay on the rocky ledge. A large limestone overhang had been the diving spot for ages. She had seen boys swing out over the ledge just missing its jagged edge to land in the water below. Many times she had held hands with one or two of her girlfriends as they ease out onto the flat rock at the coaxing of their boyfriends treading the reserve and with screams of delight and fear, jump off hand in hand.

June stretched out her legs and let the water run over them. The coolness quickly eased the burning. She wanted to slip off the rock's edge and land in the deep water below cooling her whole body in the water's comfort. Fear was the only thing keeping her from doing it. The night was growing darker and she had never swam alone day or night. She knew the risks. And never being one to take risks, she was surprised that she had made it as far as she had tonight. It was then she realized she no longer heard Jimbo's voice in her head. She didn't hear anything but the sounds of the night.

Crickets chirping out their weather report of the night's heat. Night birds calling across the vast wooded curtain separating the river and town repeating secrets they had heard during the day. And the water with is low harmony rushing around her as she intercepted its journey. Lost in the moment June had no idea she was being watched.

Across the flat rock, on the other side of the river stood Sonny Price. He had spent the day doing chores trying to rid his mind of the call to go home. It had been riding him hard. Chewing at his ears like a gnat and he needed to rid himself of the idea. It was too soon. If it was an option at all. He needed to cool his brain from the heat of the day and the heat of the idea of going home. Two steps from the flat rock he saw June sitting in its middle. Had he stepped out onto the rock or said anything at all she could lose her footing and fall. He couldn't risk it. She had been kind to him and he owed her that much. Sonny was forever feeling like he owed everyone never feeling like he had paid his way in life. A debt too large to carry hung about his neck and he didn't know why. He knew the rumors. He had heard them all his life. How his mama, or the woman he thought was his mama, was won in a card game. How his daddy ran off. How, like his mama, he was nothing more than a poker chip to be bet and lost. How if it wasn't for the handouts he wouldn't have nothing in this world. Truly, he carried a debt too large for any man to pay.

The silence and solitude was quickly disrupted when like a couple of birddogs running down a scent, Goldie and Florence broke through the woods and the darkness shouting for June. Startled by the sudden noise, June jumped up to stand and lost her footing on the slippery rock. Without any forethought of being seen or caught, Sonny rushed out to her on the rock.

"Stop! Be still!" Sonny said. His shout flushing a murder of crows from their roost.

June screams as the quiet night erupts in shouts from all

sides.

"Who is that?" "You get away from her!" Goldie and Florence riddle the stillness with frenzied accusations.

"Easy now. If you can ease down on all fours that would be best. Can you do it?" Sonny coaxes June with his calming voice trying to quell her fear and ignoring the two women on the other side of the river.

"That's it. Don't worry about them. I'll get you off there. Just move slow and easy. That's it." Sonny coaches as June measures each movement to his words. She can't see Goldie and Florence. Their voices swell in pitch behind her but she knows they have not moved from the edge of the water. Worried they would have tried to rescue her from the water or from Sonny, she decides to concentrate solely on Sonny and getting off the flat rock before the water or her misstep sends her over the edge.

Sonny takes two more steps closer to June. Easing down to help her to a standing position he grabs her arms just as she recoils in pain. The firm grasp of his large hands connecting with her tender sunburn felt as if her skin was being peeled from her flesh. Her jerking back and his grabbing forward sent both of them over the flat rock's edge into the blackness.

Goldie and Florence stood gasping for air as the sight of June and Sonny disappearing rendered them speechless. On cue the sound of barking dogs off in the distance brought them back to the moment. As if reading each other's minds they turn to rush back through the woods to Goldie's waiting car and Ruskin.

Separating at Goldie's house, Goldie rushes to the car and Florence rushes to the phone. She calls the police station and reports what has happened. Goldie bruising the heel of her hand on the car horn summonsing Florence. Its motor revving as Goldie waits on the street in front of Florence's house.

Paying no heed to marked speed limits, Goldie speeds through town and out the state highway that leads to the boat access on the river. Passing cars are colorful blurs as she steadies the steering wheel with one hand while pumping the car horn with the other ignoring the pain in the palm of her hand. Florence helps by navigating watching the road behind and up ahead while waving her arm out the window when needed. Like moths to the flame, curious by-passers join in the rally, Arvis Ange being one, and within minutes the river's dirt access road is packed.

Cars and pickups scramble for parking as everyone rushes to follow Goldie and Florence. Others run out in front of them surmising something has happened at the swimming hole. Ruskin's police car can be heard in the background of shouts and calls to join in to help.

Two or three handfuls of kids, June's age, jump in as soon as they see the two swimming to shore. By the time they all make it to the bank, Ruskin has made it down to where Goldie and Florence are waiting. Arvis is waddling behind Ruskin doing his best to make it there in time.

"June! You alright?" Florence asks. Panting as she helps lift her out of the water.

"Yes, ma'am." June says with a cough.

The crowd stands like statues as Sonny Price rises from out of the watery darkness. Dripping wet he stands ready to face his accusers.

"Son, you okay?" Arvis asked pushing through the crowd.

Sonny nods and keeps his head tucked certain he is about to suffer a fierce onslaught of incrimination. From his vantage point, it appears everyone from Fulton, down the ridge, and Tillman have turned out to see what was going on at the river.

"Sonny Price!" Goldie shouted her voice filling the space above everyone's head as she announced the obvious.

Seeing that June was unharmed, Goldie pushed everyone aside to get to where Sonny was standing at the water's edge. Arvis reached out to help her make it across the gnarled roots, river rock, and water soaked ground. Like parents concerned for a wayward child, Arvis and Goldie took inventory of Sonny's condition and offered comfort.

"You alright? Nothing broke is it?" Goldie asked. Peppering him with questions like a mother hen.

"Leave the boy be, Goldie. Can't you see he's alright? Why that boy's been jumping off there and swimming these waters since before he could walk." Arvis said giving Sonny the once over making sure nothing was broken or out of joint.

Sonny stood still unsure when the two would pounce sending him on his way to the damnation that was his due. A chill captured the attention of the two caretakers and they insisted he get out of the wet clothes and began arguing between themselves where this should take place. Arvis almost confessing he had been caring for the boy since winter nursing him back to life and Goldie almost confessing she had been secretly jealous for missing out. Florence stood by watching the spectacle and offered that they all return to her house.

The onlookers disbursed as quickly as they arrived leaving the rest to return to town two by two. With Sonny safely in the cab of Arvis's truck, Goldie turned her attention to June. Florence and Ruskin were the first to arrive back in town and she filled the percolator while Ruskin pulled together a change of clothes for Sonny. Goldie and June pulled in across the street and joined the others after June had a quick shower and change of clothes.

On the way to town, Arvis convinced Sonny it was time to go home. He offered to drive him there after they had a chance to pay their respects at the Bright's. No need starting his new life off on a bad foot by not stopping for a quick cup of coffee with the ones that saved his life. Sonny agreed knowing he had been given a second chance at making a life for him and his family. Whatever happened going forward he knew the debt he had been carrying around with him had been washed clean when he came up out of the water tonight.

It appeared to him that the whole town had turned out to see the dead rise from the deep. And, unlike what he had expected for the last several months, no one was there to accuse him. He was met with love and forgiveness and now it was time to forgive himself. It was time to go home.

Chapter Thirty-two

The sky stretched out like a blue blanket as far as the eye could see. The church bells rang as its members rolled out of shiny cars the last of the summer's heat floating like radio waves across the churchyard ready to report the news.

Women in brightly colored dresses with matching handbags and shoes fussed over their children's cowlicks and crooked bangs while their husbands snuffed out cigarettes under the toes of polished shoes.

Brother Bardstrom Strap stood at the church's open door beaming, welcoming the crowd inside. Men with their white shirtsleeves rolled up to their elbows and sweat stained hat bands waved a stream of cars to the open lot beside the church used this morning for overflow parking.

Decorations from last night's wedding filled the pulpit and windowsills as hushed conversation filled the pews. Bodies pressed in shoulder to shoulder making room where none existed for just one more to squeeze in at the end. Red faced deacons scrambled in the back of the sanctuary unfolding metal chairs creating new rows. No sooner had one row filled another was needed. No one had ever witnessed such a turnout. Nothing rivaled it.

As Brother Strap stepped onto the platform, the choir stood and began singing Amazing Grace. The congregation coming to its feet joined in drowning out the organ with their voices. It would be talked about for years to come how no one could ever remember a service such as this.

June sat twisting her wedding band around her finger with Jimbo's arm draped around her shoulders. She was so proud to see their wedding decorations held up overnight and looked as pretty in the morning light as they did in candlelight. No one expected them to stay over for the service but they both said they wouldn't miss it for the world.

Across the aisle from the newlyweds sat Arvis Ange and

Goldalena Filbry looking as proud as two people could be in church. Arvis in his only suit, two sizes too small, and Goldie in her best-polished cotton dress and matching hat. The Hatch family, Ellis and Virginia, and each of the sisters and their husbands took up three rows. Virginia battled the heat and morning sickness in silence. And behind them, were Ruskin and Florence Bright looking a bit out of place in the Baptist church, but the Bright's like so many others were determined to be in attendance for today's service.

All eyes looked up from their hymnals as the last chords drifted from the organ's pipes and out the open doors where the men with the rolled up shirt sleeves congregated on the church steps. As the church fell silent and anticipation grew with the flutter of paper fans, Kathleen Price stood from her seat on the front pew, her baby girl cradled in her arms sleeping like an angel. Just behind her, his hand lightly pressed against the small of her back, her husband, Sonny Price.

Meanwhile, no one knew Tinkum Price had returned to the cave on the bluff. The hard earth beaten firm from rain and baked by the sun, now pitted and pocked from the holes he dug. No one knew the treasure he came to dig up, to give to his son, to end the strife and seek forgiveness.

All morning Tinkum dug one hole after another relying on his feeble memory to know where he had buried his only keepsake of a life and love lost. Tired and sweat soaked, he decided to retrace his steps hoping it would jog his memory and dislodge the burial place.

The bluff had become a sacred place for him. There in the mouth of the cave, he sat within feet of the resting place of the one thing he held dear to him. The one thing she gave him before she left this world forever. The other he joined to it when he left without a word of explanation. Fearing he would lose it, he decided almost two decades ago to give it a resting place and it was only fitting it would be someplace he felt the safest.

Walking down the outcropping of rocks set into the hillside, Tinkum turned using the shovel to steady his feet and walked back up to the top of the bluff. Like scales falling from cloudy eyes, the years were wiped away and he remembered where he buried his heart's treasure.

Squatting with the folded handkerchief in his dirty palm, its embroidered edges faded with age, he unfolded it to see the blue ribbon holding the small lock of braided strawberry blonde hair and wrapped around the top of the braid just below the ribbon's knot, a tiny curl of fine baby's hair. His dirty fingers gently traced the outline of the braid and the curl while his mind traced the time lost.

Church bells pealed in the distance as Tinkum lost his footing on the bluff's edge as he stood. Falling and tumbling over and over again against the rocks before landing face down in his watery grave, his hand opens freeing his life's treasure. The blue ribbon with its strawberry blonde braid and blonde baby's curl dance on the water's surface.

The End

Acknowledgments

Hemingway said, "Writing is...a lonely life." With that in mind, it is with much appreciation and gratitude that I thank those individuals that breached the divide keeping me from being and feeling lonely during the writing of this trilogy. Your unflagging encouragement and enthusiasm sustained me when I found it the hardest to keep going.

Had it not been for Michael W. Sheridan, Lisa E. Peerman, Albert J. Bart, Sharlean Graybill and Camille W. Blasingame, I would have been just another artist in Nashville with a day job chasing a dream. I'll never be able to repay the countless times Candice L. Reed and Paul B. Cogswell asked with deepest sincerity about my writing. Listening and enjoying as I prattled on about working through plots and character development. And, for not thinking me too crazy, when I would say how I was looking forward to seeing what the characters were going to do next.

To the four most faithful friends, supporting me throughout my life, possibly knowing long before I did the stories that lived within me would soon find their way out, Susan M. Taplin, Mary M. Baker, Christie Rice and Deborah S. Wright, I love you and thank you for believing in me long before I believed in myself.

To the man that literally sat beside me through it all, my husband Joey, thank you pales in comparison to what my heart feels. To my sons, J.P. and Tip, and their beautiful wives, Francesca and Erin, your individual and collective contributions will forever be remembered and recognized. To my cousin, Darrell Rogers, your thoughtfulness is beyond measure. And, a special thank you to my parents, the late Leon Rogers and Nancy E. Rogers for giving me more than enough to fill these pages.

And, at risk of repeating myself, I would like to say thank you to those that call the Highland Rim home. Although this is a work of fiction and no character or place is a pure reflection of anyone or anyplace in particular, I pray you find bits and pieces of yourself and the places we've called home within the stories I write – and cherish them as much as I do.

Thank you